D1475764

LADDER IN THE MOON LIGHT

Ana Ingham

Pen Press Publishers Ltd

Published in Great Britain by
Pen Press Publishers Ltd
25 Eastern Place

Brighton

BN2 1GJ

ISBN 978-1-906206-35-2

Cover painting *A summer picture for Aysel* by Bryan Ingham

Ana Ingham was awarded two literary prices in Turkey, she won the Gunter Grass and Worpswede fellowship in Germany, Yaddo in New York and was chosen Hamburg City poet. She settled in Cornwall in 1987 and was married to the painter and sculptor Bryan Ingham.

Other novels published by the author under the name Aysel Ozakin:
Flying Carpet (published by Can in Turkey, Rowohlt Verlag in Germany and Ambo in Holland)
The Prize Giving (published by Yazko, Luchterhand in Germany, Shalom in Holland, Women Press in England)
Soll ich hier alt werden (Bartelsman)
Die Blau Vogel auf dem Stirn (E and Luchterhand)
The Langue of the Mountains (By Luchterhand and Bartelsman in Germany, by Ambo)
Die Blau Maske (by Can in Turkey, Luchterhand in Germany, Ambo in Holland)
Galube Liebe Aircondition (Luchethand and Goldman)
Three Colours of Love, The English Dream, By the Lake, Aroma of Croissants by Waterloo Press.
La Langue des Montagnes (L'Esprit des Peninsules, France)
Le voyage a travers l'oubli (La Societe des Poetes Francais, France)

Her two plays (Astronaut from Finland and Snowy Night) were performed during the 2007 Brighton Festival Fringe.

LADDER IN THE
MOON LIGHT

1

A letter from Ben, his childish scribbling so unmistakable. 'Local' was written in a corner of the yellow envelope, one of the envelopes he had bought in great quantities while they were still married. When the divorce proceedings were going on, he had taken away a pile of these envelopes together with his belongings. Now they both used the same envelopes.

In his letter Ben said he was not well, the doctor had given him some painkillers. Suzan interpreted this as a call for attention. She had not spoken to him since their divorce, crossed the street whenever she saw him. But when he phoned from the pub and asked if he could call in, she found herself blushing with sudden excitement.

"Give me half an hour," she said "I'm in the middle of something."

She wasn't. But she didn't want him to see her in everyday clothes, her hair uncombed. So, she rushed upstairs to change. She put on her navy blue knit skirt and red fisherman jumper. She brushed her hair making waves, the way she knew he would like.

He announced his arrival with his usual whistle, a whistle like a birdsong. One of his peculiarities she had missed despite her grudges. And when she saw him standing on her doorstep in his old Irish tweed coat and cloth cap, a playful gleam in his weary eyes, she felt warmth. But she received him formally, and showed him into the living room as if he were a stranger. He gazed around, searching for clues about her new life. But he was well-mannered, waiting to be shown. Suzan pointed to the armchair facing the fire where he always sat. She asked him what he would like to drink.

"I have white wine in the fridge."

"No, thank you."

She sat on the armchair opposite him. In the silence that fell their eyes met. She did not reciprocate his tender smile.

"May I smoke?" He took out a Marlboro.

She nodded. He would smoke anyway. She put an ashtray on the coffee table.

He asked whether she had been away.

"I met Nelly at the grocery shop and she said you were in Paris."

"Yes, I spent the whole of January in Paris."

He gave her an inquisitive look but refrained from asking further questions.

"I have done a lot of sculptures," he said with sudden glee, "You must come and see them."

She nodded vaguely.

"Do you stay at Tamarisk sometimes?" she asked.

'No." He gave her a forbidding look.

She got up and fed a heavy log into the fire. She was tense, remembering how she had found the lock changed at Tamarisk, his old cottage on the moor where they had lived, and how peeping through the windows she had seen a framed photograph of a woman on the mantelpiece. She suddenly regretted his presence.

"So, what's wrong?" she turned a cold face to him, "Have you seen a doctor lately?"

"Yes."

"And?"

He dragged deeply on his cigarette and spoke behind the veil of the smoke, "I have cancer."

She was speechless.

"I have been in the hospital last night and had a minor operation." He went on, "But I didn't feel anything. Local anaesthetic. I told the surgeon it was like the time I read a piece for Radio 4, when I was a student in London. I thought it was only a rehearsal, but the technician told me he had already recorded me." His weary eyes lit up with a faint smile, "I made friends with a woman doctor. She is very nice. When she was without her white coat, I was amazed at how young she was, and how beautiful her figure. We had a nice conversation. She knows about art. She gave me her private telephone number. I think she has fallen in love with me." He put his half smoked cigarette onto the ashtray.

Suzan, reminded of his flirts while they were married, stiffened.

"I hope I can manage five years," he resumed sadly but firmly.

Suzan nodded.

"The treatment can be nasty," his expression turned bitter, "My hair will fall out and I'll become ugly."

Looking at him intently, Suzan recalled how fond she was of his fine face, and how she liked ruffling his lush hair. Suddenly tears rushed to her eyes.

"Sorry," she whispered, afraid he would not like her crying face, since he always wanted her to look beautiful.

"I asked the undertaker whether there is any space near my mum and dad's grave," he suddenly adopted a humorous tone, "but the undertaker told me they will soon turn the land next to the cemetery into fields, and that my mum and dad's graves are just on the borderline. So I must hurry up if I want to get a grave there." His eyes widened and he gave a brief giggle.

Suzan wished she could resist his charm, even now.

"Shall we go to the pub and have a pasty?" he suddenly offered as if they were still living together. "I haven't eaten anything for two days. Yesterday I only had a single grape and vomited all day!"

Overcome with sadness, Suzan looked down, then said. "Okay. Let's go to the pub."

As they crossed the road, above which the illuminated Christmas decorations were still hanging though it was now February, he took her hand. Suzan was pleased by his touch. She always liked his touch.

In the pub they had Guinness. Usually Ben would stand at the bar and talk to as many people as possible. But now he wished to sit in a dim corner, just the two of them. They talked about books they had recently read, radio programmes they had heard and they knew they both liked. Regret crept up inside Suzan, remembering how much they used to enjoy each other's company when in harmony.

"I can't finish this beer," Ben left his half-empty glass on the table, "I feel sick. Do you mind if I go?"

"No." She got up too.

"No, you stay." He touched her arm. "Talk to people."

"Okay," she murmured.

He held both her hands and kissed her lightly on the lips, aware that they were being observed.

2

An owl's cry woke Suzan that night. For a moment she thought that if he died, she might die too. She also may have cancer. She felt as if he had sprinkled the dust of death over her. Was it because of his ability to draw her always into his own reality?

No! She kicked the duvet off and left the bed. She walked to the window and lifted the lower sash. A gust of wind blew on her hot face. It smelled of wet grass. Staring at the clustered houses and trees outlining the dark sky, she decided to stick to her plan and sell the cottage. She must leave this house full of memories. She must leave behind the thick granite walls, the damp ceiling, the rusted Rayburn, and the broken door handle he had smashed in one of his fits of aggression.

3

The following Sunday was bright and silvery for February and Sharon called in. Sharon had cleaned for them and now continued to do so for Ben.

"Ben wants me to take you to his studio in Trepart," Sharon said, in her robust voice. "He is giving a party, showing off his pictures to his friends."

Sharon had dyed her hair red, Suzan noticed as they crossed the street to get into Sharon's red Vauxhall.

Driving along the lanes Sharon talked emphatically about the dramatic outcome in her relationship with Simon, a window cleaner, frizzy-haired like herself.

"He kept telling me I was the woman of his life. 'One loves truly only once. I like my wife, but I love you.' That sort of stuff. And I, idiot, believed him. I was ready to spend the rest of my life with him. But then... Bastard! He's gone back to his wife! And she called, 'I bloody well don't want to be a single parent, I want him back,' she said. Then Simon phoned, 'I can't hurt my children.' 'Oh, for God's sake!' I said, 'Go back to your wife and your children and leave me alone!' Goddamn it! I was really upset. But he still phones me sometimes at six in the morning, before he goes out to clean windows." Sharon chuckled sarcastically, "'I miss you so much,' he says, 'We've got to do something about it.' 'I miss you, too, darling,' I say."

"We passed the turning to Ben's, Sharon." Suzan interrupted Sharon's stream of speech.

They drove back and took the narrow lane bordered by high hedges. All around were fields and meadows of different shades of green, and the undulating hills in the distant haze. Suzan thought that Ben, who had ridden so many times on his old bike along this lane, might soon be gone and that this lush land would miss his admiring eyes. The painter's eyes. She, too, will miss the painter's admiring eyes. But will she miss the man who had destroyed love in her?

Many cars were parked around his studio, a converted barn next to Betty's fine house, and the white cotton curtains were drawn although it was a bright day. A sign that he had already turned his back on the world?

On opening the door, Suzan remembered that wet, windy afternoon when she had come here without warning and he had accused her of intruding into his privacy.

Her own bitter voice echoed in her ears now: 'I'll curse you! I'll curse you!'

Sharon walked into the studio; Suzan, overcome with a sense of guilt, followed hesitantly.

The studio was full packed. Large oil paintings hung on the walls and among them many portraits he had made of her. Ben, dressed in his grey jersey and mustard corduroy trousers, was talking with Betty, his landlady. Betty had aged over the last two years, Suzan noticed. Her short auburn hair showed more grey. But she was dressed girlishly, black leggings and a bulky grey jumper. Betty was never dressed elegantly but always casually and girlishly as if to advertise her American sense of comfort.

Seeing Suzan, Ben smiled faintly but did not leave Betty's side.

"The coats here," he pointed to the table next to the door.

How calculating! Suzan thought, with rising anger. He doesn't want Betty to think he still loves his ex-wife. But she went over to him and kissed him fondly on the cheek.

"How nice to see you again!" Betty received Suzan in faked enthusiasm. They had never been really friends. And Suzan had always sensed Betty's lingering hostility. She was of course jealous. Once Suzan had asked Ben if Betty was in love with him. He shrugged, 'Don't know. She never said so.

Anyway she is too old to be a lover and too young to be a mother.'

Although he was well known for his generosity, there were no snacks this time, but a few bottles of wine. Suzan knew why. His bank statements were still coming to the cottage, and she had opened one of them. He was overdrawn. He spent so much money converting the barn here at Betty's and another one in town, refurbishing both of them with handmade wooden furniture, stained glass doors, antique chairs... He always reshaped and embellished the places where he dwelled and inspired others to do the same. Why doesn't anyone buy a painting now? Suzan thought resentfully.

"I don't understand his paintings, I just look at the colours," said Mr Rower who owned a third of the shops in town.

Preoccupied with drinks and chats, the guests hardly looked at the pictures. Perhaps his pictures intimidated them and challenged their visual habits. But a couple of art students showed enthusiasm and asked him questions about his pictures. Ben talked to them affectionately, respectfully. Observing him Suzan felt admiration. How dedicated he was! How truly artist! He never really sought the praise of critics but strove to influence ordinary people; farmers, workmen, shopkeepers, travellers, cleaners... Some of them were here now and he gave his attention to each equally.

"Look, you are everywhere!" Sharon exclaimed, swivelling her hand toward the portraits.

"Yes," Suzan smiled and felt grateful for the portraits he had made of her.

Anthony came in with June, his ex-wife. Why on earth had they come together? Suzan wondered. June dressed neatly in white, her silky fair hair flowing on her delicate shoulders, looked as usual angelic. But why on earth did she break out of her marriage after thirty odd years and run off with another man? And was Anthony still attached to her?

Anthony had lately been calling in at the cottage for a chat and Suzan sensed his interest. But accustomed to Ben's fiery seductiveness, she did not know what to make of Anthony's modest signals. Since her divorce she had not been with another man and feared that she would never again be able to fall in love. But over the last few weeks she found herself warming up to Anthony. She had known him for several years, first as Ben's friend, then meeting him here and there, by chance. But he remained a mystery to her. Even when he chuckled, his brown eyes remained guarded, and the hollowness beneath his prominent cheeks hinted at sadness. Yet there was something appealing about him.

Leaving June with the other people, Anthony crossed the room to come over to Suzan. He kissed her on the cheeks and said with a touch of irony: "I didn't know he had painted so many portraits of you." Suzan wondered again if Anthony was jealous of Ben's talent. Once she had asked him what he thought of Ben's painting. "I don't think my pictures inferior to his," he had replied, "I find his pictures too complicated."

Before returning to June's side Anthony asked Suzan if she would be in on Wednesday afternoon.

"Yes," said Suzan.

4

"I cried the other day when someone asked me in the street about Ben's illness. I was so embarrassed," Suzan told Anthony as they sat in the dim kitchen, near the lit Rayburn. It was the warmest corner in the cottage. Outside was grey and windy and Suzan was feeling lonely. She had hardly any close friends in town. They seemed rather suspicious of Suzan after her divorce. They knew she had been the one who had wanted the divorce and perhaps they thought she had no reason to remain in their town, as she was not local.

She was dressed carefully for Anthony's visit: a dark green skirt highlighting her delicate roundness, her lush brown hair pinned loosely on top of her head.

"You shouldn't be embarrassed." Anthony bent toward her and the old wooden chair on which he sat creaked, "Of course you are upset."

"I'm not only upset about his illness…" she said, running her hand along the brass edge of the Rayburn, "but also because… because he destroyed something very valuable… between us…"

"But when you weigh his good and bad sides," Anthony cut in, "I'm sure you'll realise his good side tips the balance."

Suzan rose and walked to the small sash window overlooking the garden. The Italian flower pots had been blown over again in the ghastly wind and the grass was overgrown. As she stared at the high stone walls hung with trellis and roses, the memory of that sunny afternoon rushed to her… Sitting on this blue bench, now ruined by too much rain, Ben, his cheeks rosy, his almond eyes sparkling with joy, pointed to the cat: "Look! she is going to dance! She is going to dance! Come on, Tabby, do a dance!"

Afraid of too much regret, Suzan turned round to Anthony. "When we were happy, we were very happy," she said. Then her husky voice tinged with resentment, "But he could not bear happiness." Her dark eyes clouded, "He created conflicts or... flirted with other women. He was manipulative. "

"Manipulative?" Anthony interrupted with a glint of irony in his shrewd eyes.

"Yes he was!" Her voice went high, then she broke off. After a moment of silence she spoke with fondness, "But as an artist, he was honest, very honest. He never compromised. He only painted what he wanted to paint. And I have great admiration for him for that." She returned to her seat. She remained still for a moment, arms folded. Then she said abstractedly, "Maybe one shouldn't expect artists to be morally very correct." She looked tentatively at Anthony, "You, maybe... are... too correct."

Anthony, slightly baffled, grinned.

"How do you know I'm correct?"

"How?..." There was silence of suspense. Then she spoke in a clear voice, "I know you're attracted to me. But you're... maybe careful... You may be thinking I'm the ex-wife of your friend. Or you may be still attached to June."

"No, no." Anthony shook his head, then joined his hands on his knee and spoke in a flat voice. "My wife and I are good friends now. And she has her own life..." He paused, his eyes in deep sockets, lost in thoughts.

Observing him, 'He is handsome,' Suzan thought. His broad shouldered and well-shaped, tall stature suggested a shield against the world and his large but elegant hands which he spread whilst speaking, stirred a desire to be touched by him.

Yet her mind interfered and eliminated the wave of desire inside her. She would not yield to her demanding body. She would not. That would be in bad taste, a kind of betrayal, though she had her justification. Since their divorce her life had been busy and orderly, translating books from French, working on and off as supply teacher and writing poems. She had a few women friends in town – Nelly and Lisa for instance, and there had been a few men who had shown interest in her and some had been insistent. She was now thirty-eight and had an intelligent simplicity that impressed perceptive men. But for some reason she had not been able to build a relationship with any of them. And now, for the first time since her divorce, she felt she could get involved. But wouldn't that be cruel while Ben was in the clutch of cancer? But why should she still be loyal to him? He had not been to her even while they were married. And six months after their divorce she saw him one summer morning walking up the road with a woman in turquoise shorts and carrying a picnic basket. Imagining him having picnic with another woman, Suzan had felt a piercing pain.

"It's not that," Anthony's deep voice broke the chain of her thoughts. She looked up to face him.

"I am careful… maybe too careful," went on Anthony, "And you're not the first to tell me that. You have been honest and I'll be honest with you. I have a problem."

"What problem?" Suzan asked abstractedly.

"The problem… I seem to be unable to take a step forward. If I take a step forward, then I take two steps back. Somehow I feel, I cannot open the door. I want to open the door, but I cannot."

"Afraid of some disaster?" Suzan fixed her piercing gaze on him, eager to challenge him. "Maybe as a child you were led to believe that people could only survive if they carefully watched their steps." She knew he was the son of a miner.

"Maybe…" he grinned with some embarrassment, "Maybe you're right. I always watch my steps." He paused and staring toward the window, he said, "I think my painting suffers from that, too. I cannot express my experiences in my paintings. Maybe because my experiences have been so painful. And I feel if I express my experiences in my paintings I will feel the same pain again."

Suzan was touched by his sincere revelations and wanted to hear more, "You mean not being able to open the door and not being able to paint the pictures you would like to paint... are linked?"

"Yes. I think so." He looked at Suzan, and spoke eagerly, "I'm hiding. I'm escaping emotions because... because I can't open the door."

"Me, too." Suzan looked him in the eyes, and after a pause said, "I cannot move on... I want to move on... I want to leave behind the past. I want to move on... Does that sound cruel?"

"No." Anthony bent towards her and looked her deeply in the eyes, "You are a free person."

Suzan felt the exchange of vibrations between them. Her eyes resting on his slightly lined forehead, she thought she could be happy with him. Happy, safe, understood. But... She looked away. Could she love him? Could she love him deeply, in the way she once loved Ben?

5

That evening, there was a call from Ben.

"I decided to take the treatment," he told her.

"I'm so glad," Suzan said.

"I asked the doctor whether I could hang on for five years."

Suzan was silent.

"The doctor said that it would be too optimistic."

Suzan bit her lower lip.

"I would like to live for a few more years." His voice trembled. But he quickly regained his self-control as he went on, "Illness brings another attitude, another set of values into one's life. And it has already."

Suzan sighed, her gaze fixed on the receiver.

"The doctor said I can drink and smoke as much as I like, because my cancer has nothing to do with drinking," Ben resumed, hinting perhaps at her warnings. "It's just God messing things up. I'm now even more of a non-believer. I'll go through the town and spray on the walls: 'Sod God!'"

"Don't say that," Suzan said with gentle voice, "I'm a believer. I believe in divine justice."

There was silence on the other end of the line and Suzan regretted what she had just said.

"Shall we go to the opening at Penzance Gallery on Friday?" Ben suddenly offered, as if to abandon the sad topic.

"Yes," Suzan replied vaguely.

"I'll ask Anthony if he can take us there," Frank said in an animated tone.

Suzan blushed, feeling as if he could see her through the receiver.

6

When Suzan saw Ben and Anthony side by side at the bar, she was struck by their differences. Not only their appearances but also their personalities seemed almost opposite. Ben, not tall, not well-shaped and worn out by his illness, still had a forceful presence. Anthony on the other hand, taller and very well-shaped, looked rather self-effacing.

June who stood next to Anthony acknowledged Suzan with a reserved smile. Suzan drew closer to Ben and kissed him fondly on the cheek.

"You're looking well."

"I'm eating every day," Ben said cheerfully.

"Maybe you've just played a trick," Suzan attempted a joke.

"Yes, I fooled the world," Ben said, a mischievous twinkle in his weary eyes.

"How typical of you!" Suzan patted on his arm.

Reminded perhaps of her accusations in the past, he gave her a bitter look, but then, he stroked her hand and asked if she would like to have a 'half a Guinness' as usual.

"Yes, please."

He downed his beer and bought a round.

"Cheers." He raised his glass first to Suzan then to Anthony and June.

Anthony and Suzan raised their glasses simultaneously.

He came closer to Suzan and said in mock reproach, "Why didn't you call in? I was expecting you."

"I thought you'd give me a ring if you wanted to get in touch," Suzan replied.

"Oh! So many people called in last week," he complained a little vainly.

"Your popularity will increase because of your illness now." Suzan brought her face closer to his.

"Yes." Ben pouted childishly, "Somebody said the other day, 'the price of your pictures will go up now'." He grinned then took a large gulp.

"But you're drinking too much again," Suzan said, tapping his belly. Then looking up, she caught Anthony's observing gaze. A nervous smile stretched his thin wet lips and he looked away.

They left the pub and walked down towards the line of parked cars, Ben and Suzan ahead. They were going to drive in June's car. Ben and Suzan approached a yellow car simultaneously, thinking it was June's. And as they grasped the handles of the doors on either side, June called out: "Not that one! My car is over there."

Suzan and Ben giggled simultaneously about this common mistake.

June suggested Ben sit in the front with Anthony.

"I'm sorry it's untidy," she picked up a pile of papers with both hands from the front seat.

"It's like an office here," Ben said.

As they drove along the winding country lanes, June began to talk about her job and about the increase of drug addiction among teenagers. June was a social worker.

'Her job suits her character,' Suzan thought, listening to June. She seemed altruistic. The kind of woman who would always smooth over imperfections and failures. But why on earth did she run off with another man? Was she alarmed by the prospect of spending the rest of her life with Anthony? Anthony would certainly live with her for the rest of his life and never run off with another woman.

When they arrived at Penzance, the seaside town populated mostly by pensioners and aspiring artists, it was already dark. Anthony stopped at the end of the lantern-lit cobbled street, in front of the gallery which was in the basement of a large Victorian house.

"What time do you wish to be collected, ladies and gentlemen?" he joked.

But his joke remained without response.

The gallery was crowded with artists, some of them dressed with a touch of eccentricity, handmade jewels, embroidered jackets, bulky trousers. There was a kind of tribal link among them, Suzan noticed. They met often at parties, and in the same pubs, joking and gossiping, but rarely talking seriously. Although they seemed proud of having moved down to Cornwall and living surrounded by the great natural beauty, they had the sadness of those who lived in exile. They were so far away from London, and their talents would perhaps never be recognized by the art world.

Ben had never quite mixed with these aspirants, yet he treated them with genuine affection, always giving them good advice, Suzan remembered. And now as the four of them entered the gallery, all heads turned towards Ben, and many stepped forwards to welcome him. Had the sad news already reached them? But he had always been the centre of attention in such gatherings. 'They are proud of knowing him,' Suzan thought, observing people who had quickly encircled him.

The paintings on the walls were the work of ordinary people who had been taught by Anthony in evening class. While Ben engaged with the artists and June joined a group of her friends, Anthony stayed by Suzan. He introduced her to a white-haired man and his wife.

"Look, this gentleman is a fisherman and now he is an artist," he said proudly.

"Do you make a living from selling your pictures?" the wife of the fisherman asked Anthony.

"I don't need much money," Anthony replied, "My tiny cottage is cheap to run and I get all my wood from the valley. June, my ex-wife, has recently paid fifty pounds for a few bags of wood. Fifty quid, can you imagine?" He spread his big hands and bent over to the wife of the fisherman. His involvement with people was so direct, and not sophisticated perhaps due to his working class background. But Ben though coming from similar background, from a village in Yorkshire, had transformed himself.

Driving back to Heathertown later, Ben seemed quite contented and sang the old song: 'Kisses sweeter than wine'. Suzan joined him and they sang together while Anthony and June remained silent. They used to sing together quite a lot, Suzan remembered, they sang in bed on those happy Saturday afternoons… As they came to the end of the song Ben turned his face round to the back seat, to smile at Suzan.

Anthony stopped near Ben's studio in Church Street. Before getting out, Ben said to Anthony, raising his finger, "See you at 'The Bell' on Wednesday, Anthony. If you are there before me, reserve a seat."

"Right, Ben. Will do," Anthony lifted his hand in a man-to-man intimacy. Then he turned his head round to the back seat to crack a joke: 'Sorry, we can't invite you, ladies." He explained that he and Ben went to The Bell to watch football on Wednesdays.

"Come along for a coffee sometime, Ben," June called as Ben got out of the car.

"Will do," said Ben. Then, through the open door of the car he brought his face closer to Suzan's and spoke tenderly. "Goodnight, sweetie."

As he crossed the dimly-lit road, Suzan's sad eyes followed him. How different he was from everybody else she knew. How sure of himself even in the clutch of imminent death.

Driving on down the main street, Suzan told Anthony to drop her where convenient.

"I'll take you right to your doorstep, lady!" Anthony said.

"Thanks," Suzan murmured.

Standing on the pavement by her door, she waved to Anthony and June as they drove off. Do they still sleep together sometimes? She wondered. And had Anthony been alone now, would she offer him to come in and perhaps stay overnight? Would she? The question hung over her head as she unlocked the door and switched on the light in the lounge. Then she stood there for a few moments, staring at the armchair where Ben always had sat

7

Sunday morning Suzan went to Ben's new studio which was at the top of Trengrouse street. She hoped they would take a walk in the country, as they used to sometimes on Sunday mornings. Yet she knocked on the heavy wooden door with some trepidation, knowing his attachment to his privacy. But he was happy to see her. "Come in," he whispered, an intimate smile crossing his pale face.

He wore his red striped Van Heusen shirt, a brown bow tie and mustard-coloured corduroy trousers. 'Does he expect a woman?' Suzan asked to herself.

He showed her to the soft green armchair. The iron stove was lit. Sculptures were lined up on the shelves, along with beautiful antique jugs, and the books that he had carefully collected and kept over the years neatly placed in the wooden bookcases. He sat in his usual armchair. He had moved this armchair from the cottage here and the upholstery was partially torn, sinking in the middle. But Ben seemed determined to feel comfortable in it. He perhaps liked the image of himself sitting in his old chair. The cat jumped on his lap and began scrutinizing Suzan indignantly. She must be remembering how Suzan had tricked her into the cage one morning, by placing a plate of fresh fish in it then delivered the cage to Sharon, who had come to collect and take it to Ben. Now the cat demonstrated her determination not to be reconciled. She turned her face away when Suzan greeted her and she nestled her head snugly into Ben's lap.

"I ate rice and scallops yesterday and I didn't feel sick," Ben announced cheerfully.

"You really look well today. Maybe it's not cancer," Suzan said.

"It's cancer. But such things come and go." Ben looked away.

Suzan knew his habit of ignoring reality. And looking at him, she saw the shadow of death in his eyes. 'Perhaps death shows first in the eyes, before taking over the body,' she thought.

Ben, eager to change the subject, pointed to the chopped vegetables on the wooden table.

"I'm going to cook lunch," he said, "Maybe the idea of a Sunday lunch will stimulate my appetite."

Suzan nodded abstractedly and gazing around a framed photograph of a woman standing under a tree caught her eye.

"Is that Iona?"

He nodded, a shadow of embarrassment crossing his face. Suzan remembered that Sunday morning when Ron, the barman at The Bell, came with his daughter to Casa Mia.

Later, Suzan heard that the girl, only seventeen, had begun visiting Ben in his studio at Betty's. She wanted to learn painting from him, although she was not an art student, but was studying management.

Now Suzan could not bring herself to ask him about that girl. And the link between that seventeen-year-old girl and Ben was to remain a mystery to her.

"Ron gave it to me the other day," Ben said as Suzan went to look closely at the photograph. Then she noticed a card near the photograph. "Ron also gave me this card. Read it." Ben said.

The card was from Ron and it read: 'Dear Ben, I hope Iona's photograph will brighten up your days'.

"Does Ron think that you're attracted to his daughter?" Suzan turned to face Ben.

"I'm not attracted to her," he said rather tensely, "But I like her very much."

Suzan sat back on her chair and said nothing.

He made coffee and served it in tiny porcelain cups.

Sipping their coffee they observed each other in silence. They were both aware that there was no chance, no time to sort old conflicts out.

"Coming here I saw the placard for Red Nose Day," Suzan said, attempting a distraction.

"Oh, I hate it, I hate it!" He crumpled his face, "All kitsch! Kitsch! Kitsch everywhere! Bad taste!"

She smiled at his anger.

"In the hospital, I noticed how badly people are dressed," he went on, "They are of course depressed, but I decided to wear my best clothes every time I go to hospital, my bow tie, my leather shoes, as if I'm going to meet the Queen for coffee."

'How resilient he is, how stubbornly an artist,' Suzan thought, feeling respect for him.

"But you know bad taste came to this country from America," he went on. "Britain was leading the fashion world till recently. The clothing industry began in this country. Beautifully cut dresses, the finest suits. Now it's in such decline. I'll show you something."

Jumping to his feet, he walked to the bookcase and returned with a newspaper cutting in his hand. It was an article about fashion, with a picture of a young man dressed in bulky, large-sized trousers.

"Look, this man leads fashion in Britain now! Look at these horrible trousers, these horrible trainers! And young people pay a fortune for such things now!"

He placed the cutting back inside the pages of a hard cover book.

"I keep it to show to my visitors," he said and left the book on the window sill. Before sitting back on his chair he smiled at her.

"Fancy a drink?" he asked fondly. "Somebody brought me a special whisky from Buenos Aires. Want to try?"

"Yes. I would love to," Suzan smiled back.

He went to the sideboard where various bottles stood and chose a crystal glass for Suzan. "I won't drink. I'm off alcohol," he said. He poured whisky into the glass and gave it to Suzan in a stylish manner.

Then they talked about the evening in the art gallery.

"It was a pleasant evening. I met people I knew," Ben said.

"But the pictures were not very good," Suzan said. "So many artists live in Cornwall, but few produce great pictures."

"They're not good artists. Good artists are always few."

"What do you think of Anthony? Is he a good painter?" Suzan asked carefully.

"No," Ben shook his head, "He is a good man, a good teacher, but not a good painter."

Suzan lowered her eyes. After a moment of silence she asked if he fancied to take a walk with her in the country.

"I'm expecting a guest for lunch," he said gravely, avoiding her gaze.

Afraid of conflict, Suzan could not bring herself to ask 'who?'

As she left, Ben decided to walk with her to the newsagent, to buy a Sunday paper.

"Do you want to see my new studio?" he asked, as they descended the wooden steps.

"Is it finished?"

"Not yet, but in a few weeks it will be."

He lead her to the granite building, across the back yard.

The skylights were already installed in the converted studio and the spotlights were fixed on the walls. There were two huge wooden tables in the middle of the room. And as in all the places he occupied, a wooden bed in old fashioned country style was built in the corner.

"I'll paint my new pictures here." Ben gestured about the room.

"It's a wonderful studio," Suzan enthused, "I feel envious. If I sell my house, I'll buy a barn and have it converted…"

His reproachful glance stopped her from finishing her sentence. And her regret tightened her chest. How could she be so tactless? How could she say she is envious?

He lead her out and walked with her to the newsagent.

8

Around nine o'clock that evening the telephone rang. It was Linda, one of Ben's so-called friends.

"Ben phoned me earlier this evening," Linda said in wistful voice, "I first thought I must come to terms with the news alone. But then I decided to share my grief with you." Linda's voice trembled, and she broke off. She was crying. After a moment of silence she resumed, "He has given me so much. He opened me up to art, to creativity. He has been the most significant person in my life. It's so difficult for me to accept that such a powerful man will die."

Yes, Suzan thought, like many others Linda was fascinated by his powerful presence, by his exuberance.

One day, a year or so after the divorce, Linda came to see Suzan and, lapsing into a woman-to-woman sincerity, she confessed her unrequited love. "I was in love with him. But I was not exciting enough for him, not attractive enough. After you two got married, I had to see him as a brother. Of course I was jealous of you. You were taking him away."

"I'll have to come down to see him," Linda said now. "I'm his executor."

"Are you?" Suzan was taken aback.

"Yes," Linda said, in gentle vanity, "He made me his executor alongside with Betty. He told me this evening... So I have to come down anyway... But I won't disturb him, I'll not interrupt his work. I know he will work till the end. He is that kind of person, isn't he? He will carry on working till the end. When do you think I should come?"

Suzan sensed Linda's expectation. And in a mood of resignation, "You can stay here," she said.

"Oh, thank you!" Linda's voice tinkled, "that's very kind of you."

Suzan was eager to end the conversation. But Linda was eager to talk.

"Have I told you about my new boyfriend?"

"No," said Suzan coldly.

"Ian," Linda giggled. "We get on well. But I don't have high expectations of him. He is not terribly exciting. But a good man. We respect each other."

The word 'exciting' struck Suzan. She knew Linda was comparing her new lover with Ben.

9

On Saturday night, as she crept along the pavement crowded with navy boys, a young man with shaved head and stinking of beer brought his face closer to hers,

"Are you going to sleep with me tonight, sweetie?"

The horde behind him burst into laughter as Suzan brushed past. She'd rather spend her time with the man who is terminally ill than with one of these grossly healthy young men, Suzan thought as she approached Ben's studio.

When she reached the dark yard, a sense of belonging overcame her. Emotionally she belonged to him, and paradoxically perhaps more than ever before. His imminent death captivated, engulfed her. She climbed the wooden stairs eagerly. She waited for a few seconds before knocking on the heavy wooden door. How would he receive her? Every time she came this question bothered her. She could not announce her visits. He had no telephone. But thank God he smiled as he stood against the light coming from the cavernous studio. He was, as usual, well dressed.

"Oh, you have a new haircut!" Suzan enthused as she walked in, "With this new hairstyle, you can seduce a new woman."

"Yes," he said coyly, ushering her, "I can seduce my doctor, Julie. She came with her mother the other day. I thought her mother is even more attractive and could be my girlfriend."

"You swine!" Laughing, Suzan pointed a finger at him.

"My doctor will be in the hospital when I'm having my operation," Ben went on when they sat by the window, "and I think that's very good. She will look after me. I told her I don't want any visitors while I'm in the hospital. I want to be the mysterious man who has no visitors. I've told everybody, 'Don't come to hospital, I'll be lying there encased in straps and tubes. So undignified! Why should you visit such a man? You can come and see me when I'm convalescing'."

Suzan remained silent.

"Have a drink," he bent toward her, eager to expel sadness. "Help yourself to the whisky. And give me my non-alcoholic drink."

"Okay." She got up.

Walking towards the cupboard, a letter on the dining table caught her eye. A dried forget-me-not was stuck on the bottom of the letter. She could only read the last words: 'Love as always. Yours.' She could not decipher the signature. A pang of pain inside her, she returned to her seat carrying a large Jameson for herself and a non-alcoholic drink for him.

He thanked her formally. He complained about having too many visitors, who come at inappropriate times.

"I shouted at John the other day, because he banged on my door at three o'clock in the afternoon. I was sleeping. 'Can any sensitive person visit somebody at this time of the day?' I said to him. I was so angry. All those drop-outs come and sit and roll up their tobacco and I'm the one who does the coffee for them, who offers drinks. They also expect me to entertain them, to cheer them up. They all sit there, with gloomy faces. They think they ought to look gloomy. When they leave, I feel exhausted. Oh, they are so insensitive. The sensitive ones write a letter or send a card. I got a letter from Sam the other day. You know Sam, my old friend who lives in Holland. He wants me to go to Holland and stay in his house. He talks about faith-healing. He says he has healed several people with faith-healing. And now he wants to try with me. For God's sake! I don't believe in such things. I am earthbound, prosaic. He is very emotional, Sam. We've known each other since we were students. Can you imagine how intense he will be when we meet now? Such emotional clutter. He says, 'We have always been best friends,' Well, I don't think he is my best friend. He is becoming more and more a mystical type. Why should I go and stay in a strange place, while I am getting all the necessary medical help here? And I'm not going to die anyway."

"That's the most important thing," Suzan said, "Your determination."

He nodded with grave eyes, then said, "The operation was supposed to be next week. But I've heard nothing from the hospital."

"Why don't you call Julie and ask?"

"The telephone box is on the other side of the street and I don't like to cross the road. They drive so fast, the buggers. I'm afraid of being overrun."

Someone so anxious to live should not die, thought Suzan.

"I can phone Julie and ask."

After a moment of hesitation, he agreed. How careful he was about asking her to do things for him now, as if afraid of becoming indebted to her.

She bent and took his hand that leaned on the arm of the chair. She shivered at the touch of the weak and yellowish hand, remembering the same hands when they were full and strong. Hands that touched with sensual intensity. Hands that had painted her portraits.

She flung herself to him and held him tight.

"Thank you," he whispered and remained stiff.

Suzan, suppressing tears, sat back in the green armchair.

As they quietly sipped their drinks, in the warmth emanating from the iron stove and in the dim glow of a Victorian petroleum lamp, Suzan suddenly felt that they could be together again. They knew each other so well. This time they would be able to avoid conflicts. They could accept moments of silence and indifference. Maybe this is the perfect time for them to love each other, because now they know they have no future. They always knew they had no future, but they tried hard to make one.

The night grew quieter. The navy boys and shop girls must all be packed into the noisy red-lit pubs now. And Suzan felt she would not exchange her seat in this studio which smelt of paint, plaster and wood for any place in the world. She would not exchange the company of the terminally ill man opposite her for that of any man in the world.

She finished her whisky, he finished his non-alcoholic drink. She was ready to go now and he was ready to see her off. They could not afford to express regrets. They both had to be in control. In control and well-equipped. He against death, she against the impending sense of loss.

Standing in the middle of the dim studio, they hugged, confirming their familiarity. The familiar warmth, the familiar smell, the familiar shape of each other's body.

The High Street was invaded by the staggering, shouting, laughing packs of navy boys and shop girls. Two policemen stood on the pavement, observing. Suddenly there was a panic as a frail young man, hardly eighteen, lurched onto the street in an attempt to throw himself in front of a car, his friends grabbed him from behind and held him down in spite of his desperate struggle to release himself from his saviours. The car stopped. A girl in a red dress and a leather-jacketed youth dragged the attempted suicide to the pavement. They yelled at him as they roughly deposited him in a shop doorway:

"What the fuck do you think you're doing, you bloody idiot? Do you want to spend the night inside?"

The young man lowered his shaven head into his knees, covered his face with both hands and began to cry.

10

Suzan phoned Ben's doctor, Julie, on her private number.

"I'm sorry to call you at this hour. But I told Ben that I would phone you. I'm his ex-wife. He needs to know when he is going to the hospital."

"I believe the appointment has been made for eleven o'clock on Friday," the soothing and reserved voice explained, "Would you mind calling the surgery and confirming this?"

"Will do. Thank you so much," Suzan said, her heart flickering.

She dreamt that night of Ben. He was meandering in a deserted street, inside a new Mackintosh and with a new cloth cap. She was running after him, calling without avail: "Wait! Wait for me!"

11

Torrential rain poured over Suzan as she huddled against the studio door. It took Ben some time to open the door as he had difficulty in turning the key. As he finally managed to open the door, he looked exhausted and apprehensive. A play was on the radio.

"I just came to tell you that the operation is scheduled for eleven o'clock on Friday morning," Suzan said hastily.

His weary face froze for a moment. "Come in." He whispered. "Thank you for coming by in such weather."

"Are you listening to the play?"

"I was, but it's getting too complicated, I'll turn it off."

As he walked to his bed to turn the radio off, Suzan noticed the slowness in his movements.

They sat in the armchairs. The silence in the hollow studio was broken occasionally by cars passing by. They did not talk for a while. Then he told her that Donna and Richard would take him to the hospital for the operation.

"Betty and Sharon have taken me to the hospital before," he said attempting a playful tone.

Suzan turned her face to the rattling window. The massive greyness outside intensified the sadness within her.

"Would you like some strawberries?" Ben suddenly pointed to the box of strawberries on the table.

"No, thank you," Suzan smiled faintly.

"I can't eat them. But I'll try to eat one. Are you sure you don't want them?" Ben went as if trying to cheer her up.

"No, really. Give them to the workmen." Coming here, she had seen the builders working in the adjacent building.

"That's a good idea," Ben nodded, widening his eyes, "My new studio is almost ready. It will be ready for me when I come back from hospital."

She wondered if he had enough money for such undertaking and whether he would have the opportunity to use the new studio.

They went together to the adjacent building to give the strawberries to the workmen. The sideboards and shelves were already installed. The two workmen thanked Ben for the strawberries, a knowing sadness in their eyes.

"I take them a piece of cake every day at tea time, but they make their own tea," he told Suzan as they were leaving the building. "Donna brought me a huge cake the other day. And I give the workmen a piece every afternoon at five, this enables me to keep the routine the whole week."

When he's gone, the workmen will remember this ritual and think of him affectionately, Suzan thought. And that's probably what he wants.

They returned to the studio. Suzan made some tea and as they sipped their tea, he told her that Linda had visited him the day before.

"Oh! Why didn't she call me?" Suzan was outraged.

"Well, she only stayed one day."

"But I told her she could stay in my house!"

"She told me she was going to call you."

"Well, she didn't. How is she anyway?"

"Very well. She will be my executor, together with Betty."

"Yes, she told me… " Suzan lowered her eyes.

"She bought me a box of healthy drinks from the health shop," Ben unaware of Suzan's feelings, went on, "Non-alcoholic drinks. When I went to see my solicitor Linda walked with me down the road. She said she wanted to go to the Post Office and that we could meet at the flower shop and have coffee together after I finished. So I went to wait for Linda by the flower shop. I was looking so shabby, standing there that I thought I might as well start acting like a flower seller and began calling: 'Two bunches of bluebells for only one pound! Don't miss it! Don't miss it! Good value, only one pound!' The boy in the flower shop was shocked."

Suzan laughed at this. As she left, he went down with her to the yard. He stood in front of her and kissed her gently and fondly on the lips. Then, holding her by the arm, he looked deeply into her eyes. Trying to suppress tears she walked on. Then she stopped to look back. He was standing there watching her with a smile. But then the smile faded and his expression turned sad and painful, as he raised his hand to wave goodbye.

12

Suzan was surprised by the knocking on her door as it was unusual for her to have unexpected visitors. Approaching the door she could tell it was Anthony, his lean face somewhat obscured by the lace curtain on the front door. Two weeks had passed since he had visited.

"Which wind flung you this way? Come in." Suzan held out her hand. But he gave her an enthusiastic hug which surprised her.

"I was cooking butter beans," she said stepping back.

"Yummy!" he beamed.

"Would you like some?"

"No, thanks. I'll have my pint in the pub shortly."

She showed him into the lounge.

"Sit there," she said, pointing to the armchair facing the fireplace which was stuffed with bunches of dry, crumpled paper, "So you can watch the unlit fire."

"Oh yeah, I can see the flames!" he took the joke further.

"Coffee or tea?"

"Whatever you are having."

She made tea, and returning to the room, asked whether he had visited Ben before coming here.

"Yes, I have. But he was bombarded by visitors, so I only stayed ten minutes."

"Who were the visitors?" she asked, putting a Chinese mug in front of him.

"Betty and the carpenter doing the studio. Then... when I was leaving, a girl came in."

"Who?" Suzan walking to her seat, stopped and turned to Anthony, eyebrows arched.

"Oh, I forget her name," said Anthony, a mischievous glint in his eyes, "She used to be his model. He did some sculptures based on her last summer. A dark-haired girl."

"Tracy?" Suzan gasped.

"Yes, that's her."

Suzan suspected that Anthony knew about the affair.

"Bitch!" Suzan muttered.

"Oh!" Anthony chuckled.

"Anyway, why not?" Suzan sat down, pouting, "He must be very sad over leaving behind such a variety of attractive women."

Anthony made no attempt to defend Ben. Instead, he said, in a testing tone, "Ben told me that you visit him regularly now."

"Yes, and I'll continue to do so…"

"Good," Anthony said in false encouragement.

"But only out of compassion." Suzan was defensive.

"Come on, come on," Anthony grinned. "You're still in love with him."

Suzan turned her face away and said nothing. They sipped their tea in silence.

"Are you going to visit him in the hospital?" Anthony asked in gentle tone.

"He doesn't want to have any visitors, but I'll visit him." She was stiff.

"I can give you a lift," Anthony said, "I can take you there and back."

"That's very kind of you." She smiled faintly.

Anthony finished his tea and rose energetically to his feet.

"Right. I'll be off now."

As they stood on the porch, they looked in each other's eyes for a few moments then he put his arm around her, then he brought his lips to hers, but Suzan skilfully averted his kiss.

13

The next evening, a little before nine, Suzan took a plate of soup to Ben.

There was no light in the studio. She assumed he was asleep. In the pitch dark, she tried to place the bowl through the cat flap, quietly. When she was about to descend the steps, she heard his melodious whistle like a birdsong from inside. She wished he wouldn't whistle like that any more. It would only make her miss him after his death and he must know the effect of his whistle on her.

The door opened slowly.

"Come in, my love," he whispered.

She followed him, still in the dark. He walked to his bed, and switched on his bedside lamp. He slipped quickly under his feather-filled duvet with a floral pattern.

"Come and sit." He tapped the edge of the bed.

He had new pyjamas on. He never wore pyjamas when they were together. He always slept naked. They both slept naked. His new pyjamas were cream-coloured with brown stripes and made him look like a schoolboy. And his face on the white pillow had a boyish expression too.

'He wants to leave this world as a child, cleansed of manhood,' Suzan thought. A wave of affection inside her, she stroked his forehead and his cheeks.

"You know what happened?" he said, like a boy reporting some events to his mum. Eyes wide.

"What?"

"I was attacked while I was having my sleep."

"Attacked? How?"

"There is an international band that goes around and attacks people who are on their list," his voice turned into a thrilling whisper. "So, I must be on their list, too. They must have done some research about me and found out that I have an afternoon sleep everyday. So today at three thirty they finally carried out their attack. Bang! Bang! Bang! The band is affiliated with the health shop, you know. They brought a box of health drinks. Linda ordered them before she left, twenty-two bottles. She had told them to put the box downstairs quietly. But they did not take any notice of her warning. Instead, they attempted to break the doorway and kill me of a heart attack."

When he finished this parody, he scrutinised Suzan to see whether she was really amused. But Suzan merely smiled, lamenting the fact that he was still desperately trying to amuse her as if to make up for his current weakness.

"I brought some soup for you," she said bending over him.

"I ate five scallops and rice at five o'clock today," he beamed.

"And do you want to try my soup? I can warm it up for you."

"No," he shook his head, pouting. "I can't eat anything now. I have a pain." He tapped his belly.

"Did you take your pills?"

"Yes. They make me sleep all the time." He looked away, then eager to escape the topic, he said eagerly, "You know Betty came today with her daughter, Nora. Nora has a beautiful son now, two years old. I got on very well with him. I gave him an orange and he ate it all. Then I showed him my cat. He liked the cat very much. Then we all went for a ride in Betty's car. A big adventure. 'What do you want to eat, Ben?' Betty asked. I said: 'scallops', so we went to the fish shop to buy scallops."

"Good," Suzan stroked his forehead. Then wanting to amuse him in turn, told him that Lisa whom they both knew, had introduced her to a man who needed accommodation.

'He is a working man, can pay his rent regularly, and you need cash,' Lisa had said. "But I refused. You know why?"

"Why?"

"Well, the man was from East Anglia and I remembered you once telling me not to trust people from East Anglia."

"Did I?" Ben widened his eyes, "Well, it's true. People from East Anglia are said to be hundreds of years behind the rest of the country."

Suzan grinned and went on: "Lisa told me that the man was working as a decorator and went to work at six o'clock."

"Does he paint in the dark?" Ben interrupted her, "If he goes to work at six…"

"He works for a company called 'Eclipse'."

"Eclipse? It's called so because he starts working at six in the morning, isn't it?"

They both giggled at this, then Suzan, feeling nostalgic about their happy days, sighed and "I'd better be going," she said. "You must go to sleep."

He gave one of his childish nods. She bent and kissed him on the cheeks and stroked his forehead again. He seemed cosy and well-organized under his feather-filled duvet, in his cotton pyjamas.

"Night-night," he called as she opened the door to the cold, gusty wind. "Bang the door, so that it is properly shut."

"Goodnight," she said, "Sleep well."

"Night-night. Thank you," he whispered affectionately. As she was by the door, she heard him call, "Shall we meet at the 'Fat Man's café tomorrow at ten?"

"Okay," Suzan replied and as she crossed the muddy, pitch-dark yard, his sweet voice echoed in her ears.

14

The next morning, Suzan put on her corduroy skirt which he had bought for her and went to the café. She frowned, finding Ben sitting with Ron. Seeing her enter, Ben beamed and rose. He kissed her on the cheek then looked at Ron expecting him to give up his seat to Suzan. But as Ron ignored him, he went to fetch a chair for her.

"You look very elegant today," he laid a hand on Suzan's shoulder with a tenderly admiring look.

"You bought this skirt for me, remember?" Suzan said intimately.

"Yes, I remember. You must have lost weight," he tapped on her belly.

This reminded her of the enthusiasm he always showed towards her body.

"I was discussing with Ron whether it is better to be in hospital or in prison," he told her in an attempt to entertain her. Ron grinned.

His comparison of prison and hospital was an allusion to the fact that Ron had been put in a jail four years ago, when convicted of rape.

"If you really want to find out, you must assault the staff or the surgeon in the hospital and get yourself taken to prison," Suzan said, taking his joke further, though reluctantly.

He smiled but sadness lingered in his eyes.

She asked him whether he had received the money from the buyer who owned him money.

"Yes. People usually want to pay their debts to a dying man," he replied.

"So you are rich now," she said, trying to be cheerful since it was what he expected, "And you can pay for our coffees."

"Of course! That will be my last grand gesture." He turned his face to the window and silence followed.

"I won't come to this café while you are in the hospital, and afterwards," Suzan broke the silence.

"But you might still see me sitting here in florescence." He grinned, turning his face to her.

When she did not react to this: "My ghost!" he exclaimed.

"Oh, don't be silly!" She gestured dismissively. "I only meant the time while you are in hospital."

He nodded, then said that he had to go to the Post Office. They rose, he went to the counter to pay and joked with the waitress leaving her a large tip. The three of them left the café. She decided to accompany him to the Post Office. Ron shook hands with him and in his mumbling tone wished him well. Then he dragged his heavy body down the street.

Suzan held Ben's arm while crossing the busy road, the thinned arm under the thick cloth of his jacket. She had not walked arm-in-arm with him since their divorce. She waited behind him in the Post Office. As he stuck stamps on the envelope, she noticed it was addressed to his solicitor. 'Probably his will,' but she banned the thought quickly. The emotions she felt for him since she knew of his illness had not been marred by such thoughts. But now, as she noticed the yellow envelope addressed to his solicitors, the question as to who will be his heir crossed her mind. Yet she decided not to ask him this.

After they left the Post Office, Ben looked very tired.

"I'll walk you home," Suzan offered.

They walked up the road in silence. Suzan did not hold his arm now. She could sense he was drained of energy and that he hated himself for this. But as they approached the studio she asked him whether he needed any help.

"No. Thank you," he said earnestly. "Everything is under control. Well-organised. I just need a rest before Donna and Richard come to take me to the hospital. Oh! I forgot; I have to buy cat food from this shop." He pointed.

Suzan waited for him outside the shop.

As they walked on, she said, "Shall I buy honey for you? Honey will give you energy."

"I don't like honey," he pouted.

At the driveway leading to his studio, Suzan said,

"Okay. I'll leave you here. You'll let me know the result of the operation, won't you?"

"I'll give my doctor your number, only your number. Other people can learn the result from you."

Suzan felt oddly proud of this privilege.

15

Anthony came the next day shortly before midday to comfort Suzan. Suzan remained aloof from Anthony's intimate hug. She was preoccupied with Ben, visualising him in the operating theatre. She made coffee and they sat in the lounge.

"It's good that you are here," Suzan smiled sadly.

He nodded thoughtfully, observing her. She looked at her watch, it was twelve o'clock.

"Poor Ben," she bit her lower lip. She imagined he would be brave till the last moment before the anaesthetic, trying to impress the doctors and nurses. And that they would all like him.

To remove herself from the haunting image of him in the operating theatre, his belly cut, she asked Anthony if he was planning an exhibition this year.

"No. I'm not planning anything this year," Anthony said, "I have many pictures I haven't shown yet in public. I'm not really looking for recognition. I paint for myself. Do you understand?"

"Yes. I understand, but I don't believe you..." Suzan replied.

He gave an uneasy chuckle.

"Go on then," he said, gesticulating.

"Any creative person seeks recognition," Suzan spoke defiantly. "And I think... Every creative person is a child who needs applause."

"I see your point." Anthony smiled, "I don't deny my ambitions, but the satisfaction I derive from painting is much more important to me than the recognition."

Suzan merely nodded and looked again at her watch.

"Do you mind phoning the hospital?" she rose to her feet, "I am too nervous to do it."

"Of course." Anthony got up and walked to the phone. He dialled the number while Suzan observed him from where she sat.

"Hello," he turned his face to Suzan inquiringly.

"Ward eleven," said Suzan rising to her feet.

"Ward eleven," he repeated over the receiver, "I'm phoning on behalf of Ben Jones' wife."

Suzan stood next to him, her heart racing, and trying to hear what the nurse said.

Anthony thanked the nurse and putting the receiver down he laid his hand around Suzan's shoulder, "He's fine," he said, his grip on her shoulder tightened as he repeated, "He's fine. Sleeping." Suzan looked at him in disbelief and suddenly she covered her face and burst into tears. Anthony pulled her against him and stroked gently her hair. She leaned her head against his shoulder and went on crying.

16

The day Anthony was to take Suzan to the hospital was the warmest day since the New Year. The sky was blue, the apple trees blooming.

Suzan was dressed in a yellow jacket and tightly fitting black skirt, a purple silk scarf around her neck.

"You look very elegant. Is it for Ben?" Anthony enthused as she opened the door to him.

Why couldn't he think that she had dressed for him? Suzan wondered. But he was right, she had dressed for Ben and hoped that he would tell her that she looked beautiful. For no one else's flattery would convince her as much as his and that she was even now in need of his enthusiasm.

After coffee in the kitchen, they left in Anthony's car. She asked him to stop at the flower shop in the High Street. She wanted to buy tulips for Ben.

Driving out of the town, she asked him where exactly the hospital was.

"Have you never been to the hospital?" Anthony gave her a side glance.

"I've never been to any hospital in Cornwall," Suzan replied, then, knocking on the dashboard, added, "touch wood."

"That's not wood, it's metal," Anthony joked and knocked on his own head, "This is wood."

Suzan smiled though sadly.

The weather turned dull when they arrived at the hospital and the building looked like an industrial estate. How displaced Ben must feel in such a building! He always hated those plain and functional buildings. But thank God there were fields and dark green trees in the distance, Suzan tried to see the view with Ben's eyes.

Leaving the car, Anthony helped her with her coat. As they walked side by side, the harmony between their strides struck Suzan. Or it was Anthony who adapted his stride to hers, something which Ben never did.

Anthony insisted he would wait for her in the café on the ground floor. She should visit Ben alone.

He gave her the magazine he had bought for Ben.

"It's about cycling," he said. "He told me he had done collages of cyclists."

"No, you give it to him," Suzan insisted, "I'll tell him you are here, I'm sure he will want to see you."

On reaching the ward, Suzan was alarmed to see Ben's bed empty. She noticed cards on the windowsill and a bunch of daffodils in a cheap vase. His cardigan and dressing gown, apparently provided by the hospital staff, were placed tidily on a green armchair.

The patient in the next bed told Suzan that Ben had been taken to be x-rayed. Suzan waited for a while in the room, sitting on the windowsill, overlooking the vast green fields. She wondered if he would have liked to paint this view.

She finally decided to go to radiology, two floors below, and she found him in the middle of the corridor, lying in a wheeled bed, a drip injected into a vein in his left hand. A young plump nurse attended him. His face appeared to Suzan whiter than ever before, drained of blood, swollen, probably as a result of the liquid and medicine he was being given through the tube.

"What a nice surprise," his feeble voice hissed seeing her, and he smiled wearily. She bent and kissed him lightly on his mauve lips.

"This is my ex-wife," he turned his face to the nurse, lifting his hand with the needle on it to point to Suzan.

Suzan stroked his humid forehead. His eyes looked darker in his colourless face, but the dignity in them was greater then ever.

The nurse left them alone.

"You're looking well," Suzan said clumsily.

"No," he shook his head, pouting, not pleased with her false remark. "They cut out a lot of stuff inside me, my liver is totally destroyed. I'm in terrible pain. I haven't eaten anything since the operation. Yesterday I had thirty-two drops of water. But I got sick. The nurse asked me how many drops of water I had drunk, I said 'three hundred and thirty-two'. The nurse was shocked. I had made a mathematical mistake, you see."

He managed a faint smile.

Two coarse-looking male nurses came up and pushed his wheeled bed into the x-ray room. Looking behind the wheeled bed, Suzan thought that he, who hated machines, now was at the mercy of the machines. He, who always made his own decisions, was now dependent on the decisions of others. How obedient he seemed now! Well-mannered and humble.

Suzan went to sit in the waiting room. Other patients paraded by, pushed in their wheelchairs, all silent, pale and drawn. Ben was brought out a quarter of an hour later, sad serenity on his face. The two male nurses pushed him into the lift. Suzan went in too. He avoided eye contact with her in the lift, as if embarrassed to be seen like that by her.

As he was placed in his bed by the window, he asked Suzan to bring a chair so she could sit down. He pointed to the corner, where there was a row of blue plastic chairs. She took one and sat by his bedside.

"People sent wonderful cards," he pointed to the cards on the window sill. "But Penny and John sent me a horrible card. Look! Such shit! A picture of an angel. I couldn't look at it, I turned it downwards. Oh, I hate it. I don't want to see Penny and John again, if they can send me such a card... It shows what they think of me. I shall probably frame it and hang it on the wall as an example of Welsh humour."

Although Suzan smiled, the rigidity he showed even now amazed her. He still judged people by their visual taste and his feelings were still dominated by his eyes. Suddenly a revolt stirred inside her and she felt impatient with him. She asked him whether he wanted to see Anthony.

"I don't feel particularly sociable, but he can come up for a few minutes," he said, a shadow of suspicion crossing his face. The idea that he might be sensing what was going on between Anthony and herself alarmed Suzan. How cruel it would be to inflict jealousy on him while he was so helpless.

She found Anthony sitting quietly in the café, his glasses on, reading the newspaper, his face bent over it. A sense of trust came over her seeing him like that. He looked so quiet and reliable. She felt she might love him. But could she start a relationship with him now, when Ben was so powerless and deprived of his seductive as well as destructive power.

17

Suzan dreamt of Anthony that night. She was walking side by side with him in a beautiful countryside and was feeling very happy at his company. They arrived at a house, which turned out to be her mother's house. They put their arms around each other and kissed. Then Suzan saw blood on his lips. But she realized that it was her own mouth that was bleeding. Anthony walked away without saying anything and disappeared swiftly around a corner.

Anthony phoned on Sunday morning. Suzan told him that she had just been thinking of him. "Telepathy," she said.

"Yes, my ears are burning," Anthony chuckled.

He asked how she was. She said she was trying to come to terms with her conflicting feelings.

"People related to a dying person usually get depressed," Anthony said in his avuncular tone.

How plausible and yet impersonal was his logic.

"What are you doing today?" she asked, hoping he would suggest they meet. The weather was warm and sunny.

"I am going to work for a while in the garden, then my daughter will come here in the afternoon. It's Mothers' Day, you know."

"Oh... Okay."

"But I shall come to town soon and call in."

His tone was irritatingly flat.

"One step forward, two steps backwards?" Suzan hinted at what he recently had told her about himself.

Anthony turned up unexpectedly the next day and gave her an emotional cuddle, then patted her shoulder as if to shield himself against a possible rejection.

At eight o'clock the same evening, Suzan phoned him.

"Is it convenient for you to talk now?" she asked and immediately added, "If not, give me a ring later."

"Yes, I'll give you a ring later, Suzan," Anthony said in an intimate voice.

"Good. What time, approximately?"

"Nineish."

"Okay."

Suzan waited for his call till nine thirty, then went to bed. The telephone rang as soon as she lay down. It wasn't Anthony but Sandra. As soon as she heard Sandra's ragged, drunken voice Suzan trembled with anger. She remembered how Sandra had asked her while the divorce proceedings were going on: 'Can I have him if you don't want him?' and had gone dancing with him.

"Sandra, I'm not feeling well, I can't talk to you right now," Suzan now said.

"I only wanted to ask about Ben…" Sandra moaned.

"But I can't talk now," Suzan snapped, "Goodnight."

That was her reprisal. She returned to bed and to distract herself she listened to 'Pick of the Week' on the radio. The phone rang at ten. She knew it was Anthony. She did not answer. The phone rang eight times.

In the supermarket the next day, Suzan ran into Sharon. Sharon wore a floral mini dress, her frizzy red hair sticking out.

"Oh, hello!" she exclaimed, then her expression turning anxious, "How is he?" she said.

"Wherever I go out in town, I am bombarded with the same question these days," Suzan moaned.

"Hah! I'm not going to ask you anything then!" Sharon walked swiftly away. Suzan stood there stupefied and feeling forsaken in this grey, remote town.

She walked back home listlessly. When the phone rang, she did not answer. She heard Anthony speak on the answering machine.

"Hello, Suzan, I telephoned last night. I wonder whether you are okay, Suzan. Bye, Suzan. See you soon, Suzan."

He repeated her name emphatically as if to express an inarticulated emotion.

In the afternoon, he phoned again. This time she picked up the phone.

"Oh, hello Anthony," she was formal.

"If you don't want to talk…" he sounded nervous.

"Not necessarily," she said.

"Okay. I just wanted to know how you are. Bye."

"Bye."

Around noon the next day Anthony showed up,

"I was concerned about you yesterday," he said when they sat in the lounge.

"I don't need your concern… I… need…" Suzan broke off. And there was silence.

"Maybe I should express my feelings more." Anthony spoke in a matter-of-fact voice. "People tell me this quite often, especially women who have felt warm towards me."

"You are also arrogant," Suzan was irritated.

"Me? Arrogant?" He smiled, "Why do you say that?"

"You are diplomatic too."

"What else? What else?"

"You always find an excuse for your visits."

"No. I don't need an excuse when I want to contact people, but I need a lot of space to express my feelings."

There was silence. Then, she looked at him and smiled tenderly: "Would you like some wine?"

"Yes, let's have some wine!" Anthony enthused, and as she left the room he cracked a joke: "Are you going to fetch it from your cave?"

"Yes," she turned her face to smile at him.

As they sipped their wine he sat on the floor next to her chair. She knew he was expecting her to sit on the floor too. That would be the beginning of what they both wanted and feared. Yet she did not move, as if paralyzed by a sense of guilt. So, they sat in silence staring towards the window and sipping their wine. Finally Anthony downed the rest of his wine and said he had to go and pick up his grandson from school. He left rather abruptly.

The next afternoon, as she was busy doing her translation work, she had a call from the nurse at the hospital, telling her that Ben had been transferred to the cottage hospital in town. Suzan left her desk immediately and, hands trembling, she chose a dress from the wardrobe. She knew the Cottage hospital was a place for dying people. Yet she felt as if she were going to an exciting meeting. Even now he still managed to inspire excitement in her. She bought a bunch of red carnations from the flower shop next to the Post Office. The hospital was approximately a mile off. It drizzled and the wind gusted. She could hardly keep her umbrella up.

The nurse at the reception, a stocky, short, white-haired Cornish woman, looked up at the blackboard to find Ben's name. And yes, there it was, his name! Suzan smiled sadly as she thanked the woman and let her lead her to room 17. The nurse opened the door without knocking. Knowing Ben's zealous attachment to privacy, Suzan hesitated before entering. Then she heard the nurse speak to him: "Here you are, love; you've got a visitor."

He was just waking up and shot a reproachful glance at the nurse. But, then on seeing Suzan, he smiled.

"Hello," he whispered sweetly.

"You shouldn't lie in bed all the time," the nurse told him in motherly authority, "You should try to sit."

He dismissed the nurse and she walked out defiantly.

"The nurses here are no good," he complained, while Suzan arranged the carnations in a vase, then he pointed commandingly, "Put the vase in front of the mirror."

She did as told, then walked to the chair by his bed. His green corduroy trousers were laid on the back of the chair.

"Can I put your trousers there?" she pointed to the foot of his bed.

He nodded sourly, not pleased with this intervention. After placing his trousers carefully at the front rail of his bed she sat on the chair and there was a moment of silence. Then as usual he attempted to amuse her.

"I was brought here in a tank, probably left over from the Second World War," he said, "Bump bump! It was horrible. Painful!"

"Do you watch this?" Suzan asked pointing to the TV screen placed near the bed.

"Of course not!" he sounded offended that she could even presume such a thing.

Looking at his pale, drawn face she felt both anger and admiration. She admired his stubbornness, his loyalty to his convictions and his principles even now, lying in a hospital for the dying. Anxious to distract him from his grim conditions and make him appreciate her presence, she told him about a funny incident she had witnessed in the pub. "John, the footballer, put up a poster of a famous football player. Then Harry, you know Harry, the guy with long white hair and beard, nicknamed 'Professor Off', because of his lectures on spiritual issues, yes, he, he stuck a sheet of paper over the poster. It was a declaration written by him in longhand, entitled: 'The Meaning of Life.' Then John, the footballer, went over to him and the two began shouting at each other. Finally they grabbed each other. Then Lisa came up and whispered into my ear: 'That must be the meaning of life.'" Suzan smiled looking up at Ben.

"That's a nice story," his face lit up.

"It's a nice room," said Suzan, pointing to the window which overlooked meadows.

His gaze hovering the distant view, he nodded.

"Have you eaten anything today?" Suzan asked.

"Yes, we had roast chicken for lunch," he said earnestly, "The only proper meal I've had for three weeks. Here the food is good. In the other hospital the food was very bad. First, you had to struggle to open the plastic clip box, then you had to smell the stale bread, cut diagonally rather than into tiny pieces, so that when you bit into it, it crumbled. Oh, it was so disgusting."

"I'll cook roast chicken for you when you're discharged," Suzan said, patting lightly on his hand resting on the edge of the duvet.

A hint of regret and nostalgia shadowed his face. He was obviously recalling as she herself did, their happy Sunday luncheons in the lounge of their cottage, wood fire burning, music by Chopin or Bruck on the radio, the black cat curled up on the floor... Perhaps to push away, the memories and regret, he said, "Trevor came to the hospital. You know Trevor, the toy maker. He brought me Jelly Pops. Look!" He pointed to the paper bag on the bedside table. "They are very good, I ate one. Do you want one too?"

"No, thank you," Suzan smiled, affection swelling inside her.

"Trevor was very sensitive, he did not stay long." He went on in his sweet voice.

"So that's your new criterion now," she smiled, "If people stay a short time they are sensitive and if not, they're stupid."

"Yes. True." He gave a boyish nod. "Sharon came too," he added, "I like Sharon because she's looking after my cat now."

Suzan remembered how he had told her in the past that he wouldn't trust Sharon because she wore horrible clothes and laughed too loudly. He always tended to judge people by their clothes and manners. But it would be absurd to analyse him now, or contradict him.

"I saw your cat on my way here," she said instead, trying to be gleeful. "She was waiting at the doorstep, watching out and looking quite grumpy."

"Hmmm…" He pouted, "Say hello to her. Talk to her, she must be feeling very lonely."

"I will," Suzan smiled. "I will talk to her and tell her that you will be back soon. Do you miss her?"

"Of course I miss her. If Anthony comes to visit me I'll ask him to take me to my studio for five minutes, so I can see my cat. If the doctor allows me to go out, that is."

"Shall I phone Anthony and tell him you are expecting him?"

"Yes. Tell him also that I liked the cycling magazine he brought very much."

"Okay, will do. I'll be off now," Suzan said softly, afraid of stirring doubts in him.

"If you wish," he murmured with somewhat suppressed sadness. "I'll walk you to the door." Leaning on his hands he sat up with difficulty and spoke in a lively voice, "I can walk now. I can walk upright, although it's much easier to walk when bent."

As he left his bed, Suzan observed him. How thin and white his ankles were now, how hollow his chest! His weight must be only a child's. And yet he radiated such pride and dignity anxious to keep his autonomy.

He put on his silk mauve dressing gown, tying the belt carefully.

"Do you want to hold my arm?" she asked, noticing his dizziness.

"No, no," he muttered. "That would mean I need help."

They walked along the long corridor, she ahead of him and she wondered whether she should let him walk ahead. Suddenly she remembered his outburst on a pavement in Worpswede where they had met while staying in Germany as visiting artists. He had yelled at her because she was walking ahead and not as speedily as he wished.

"Gosh! How long this corridor is!" she heard him say with a weary exclamation. "I've never been here before."

Touching his arm gently, she led him towards the exit.

"Do you want to rest here for a moment?" she pointed to the bench against the wall.

"I might," he said quietly, "after I see you off."

He walked a few steps toward the waiting room on the other side of the corridor. Then, noticing a corner with colourful toys for children, he said in a childish enthusiasm, "Look! I can play with these."

His joke touched Suzan deeply, and she thought: yes, he has gone through life like a child, and now he wanted to die like a child.

Reaching the exit he held gently her hand and looked at her face with a romantic admiration, then he kissed her lightly on the lips. She disguised her reluctance. His drained lips had the taste of death now.

"Shall I come again tomorrow?" she asked.

"Come whenever you wish. But come for fun, not because you feel you ought to."

Damn! He still wanted to determine the way she should feel! How could he expect her to come to him 'for fun' at the hospital reserved for dying patients?

He stood in the middle of the landing to wave to her. He looked so small and yet so powerful! She turned twice to wave back, reminded of the game they played when they were happy and in love.

18

Suzan was running along a vast, sandy beach, the sea shimmering under silvery light. A shepherd was running beside her. The beach was deserted, Anthony was in the distance. She kept running towards him and thinking: 'I shall love him. I shall love him.' With these words, she woke up and reflected upon her recurring dream. Would they ever be able to overcome ambivalence and reach a consent for a life together? A stable life free from stormy emotions…

She phoned him up.

"I'm just cooking pasta," said Anthony, his tone hinting at a reassuring and earthbound life.

"Can I come to see you tomorrow morning?" Suzan asked.

"Of course you can! But I promised my neighbour to plant trees with him in the morning."

"Then I shouldn't come…"

"No, no! I didn't mean that." He sounded anxious to see her. "What time are you planning to come?"

"There's a bus which arrives at your village around half past ten."

"All right. I'll be planting trees between nine and half past ten."

The next day was sunny. When she arrived at the whitewashed cottage, nestled on the edge of a winding country lane, she found the front door open. She called, then she peeped in. Nobody was there. She assumed Anthony was still busy planting trees.

She needed to go to the toilet, so she went inside. She had come here with Ben once. Anthony and June were still together then. It struck Suzan that the place was as clean and tidy as when June lived here. And the same family photographs were still hanging on the walls of the lounge and also of the bathroom. As she was still there, she heard Anthony call for her.

"I'm in the bathroom!" she called back.

She returned to the parlour and found Anthony placing kindling wood into the tiny range. He wore a fisherman smoke and his tanned face radiated strength and clarity.

He made tea and they sat on either side of the range on two wicker chairs. She told him that the bus passed through several hamlets which she didn't know existed; it was a rundown bus, rattling and creaking.

"And the driver looked rather like a hooligan. Broad shouldered and long haired.'

"Like me?" Anthony grinned.

"A bit," Suzan giggled but she wished he didn't have such a plain sense of humour.

"Would you like to take a cliff walk?" he asked her.

"Yes, that would be nice!" She got up.

"But first I'll have a quick wash."

He went to the bathroom. A few moments later, he came out topless, drying himself with a small towel. She felt slightly uneasy seeing him like that. His body, slightly muscular and well-shaped, seemed somewhat mechanical.

He came closer to her, still drying himself. He smelt of earth and soap. For a moment she felt excited. But then irritation replaced excitement. Suddenly Anthony's healthy body seemed to her like an unfairness, thinking of Ben's frail, dissolving body, which used to have such vibrant, intimate vitality. Anthony's statuesque body lacked that vibrant vitality. She looked away. Then she heard him say in a robust voice, "Do you want to see my pictures?"

"Yes," she nodded.

He led her to the sitting room, furnished with a floral seventies suit, conventional and comfortable.

As they stood side by side looking at his pictures, he glanced at her to see her reaction. The paintings showed meadows and trees in faded green and grey colours. She found them melancholic. Suddenly a small picture caught her eye: "Ben's!"

Anthony nodded somewhat coldly. She was so strongly absorbed by Ben's explosive and adventurous abstract painting, that she hardly looked at Anthony's large landscapes. There was not an outburst of joy or rage in them. They were predictable like his sense of humour and his well-shaped body, which, Suzan sensed, was waiting for her touch.

Anthony must have sensed she was comparing him with Ben. He left the room quietly and returned wearing a grey trousers and a navy blue T-shirt.

He led her to the cove, then to the cliff. The landscape was overwhelming. Lush green fields, rocky cliffs, the zigzagging shoreline, the shimmering ocean. All was just like in her dream, except that there was no happiness inside her.

Anthony pointed to a cove.

"In summer, I swim there every day. I jump from the cliff."

He greeted a couple, who walked past them.

"Now the whole village will know," he said afterwards. "They'll gossip. They will say: 'Anthony walked with a foreign woman.'"

Her heart sank at this joke.

Walking on, he showed her a hidden corner behind the bush where some driftwood was piled, wooden posts smoothed and bleached.

"These are mine!" he said, "I gather them and keep them here where nobody can find them, then I take them home bit by bit."

Suzan suddenly felt very hot.

"It's very hot, I must take one of my pullovers off," she said.

He stood at a distance, watching her as she took her pullover off.

"Is that all?" he teased her.

Suzan remained aloof. Arriving at Cadgwith Cove, they climbed down the hill, strewn with whitewashed cottages, in their gardens daffodils, bluebells, primroses, narcissus and lilacs. He led her to the pub perched on a terrace. They sat on the wooden seats outside. He bought Guinness for them. They clinked and sipped their drinks in silence for a while. But all of a sudden tears rushed to Suzan's eyes. She cried maybe because she felt she could not love Anthony, or any man... Any other man than the man who was dying.

"You are depressed," Anthony said. Then he took her hand in both of his and stroked it tenderly. It was for the first time that he expressed his affection towards her so openly.

She withdrew her hand carefully, and wiped away her tears with the clean handkerchief he handed her.

"Maybe I should go to Paris for a while," she said, "My poetry collection will be out in a week's time."

"Yes, go to Paris," Anthony squeezed her hand. "You have to promote your poetry book and it would do you good."

"But how can I leave Ben now?"

"You are no longer his wife," he snapped, "You must get on with your own life."

Then he brought his face closer to hers and said, "Fancy another beer?"

"I'll get them," Suzan said, rising, and went inside the pub.

They sat for a while, quietly sipping their drinks and staring towards the sea. Then Suzan broke the silence, "I know you are a good man," she smiled faintly. "And I desired you sometimes."

"We shouldn't take a walk then, I should show you my bedroom," Anthony offered with a grin.

Suzan looked down and said no more.

When they finished their beer, she asked him if he could take her to town.

"Of course. I'll be a gentleman," he said his robust voice hiding sadness.

As they drove up along the country lane, he became light-hearted again. He pointed to the garden with its tiny pine trees newly planted.

"Look! My neighbour and I planted them. That is what I was supposed to be doing today. But then you came."

"But now you have planted a friendship." Suzan told him, wanting to end the ambiguity.

He kept staring into the distance, a fading smile on his square face.

19

Arriving at the hospital the next day, Suzan found Betty sitting on the visitor's chair. Ben glared at her implying she had come at the wrong time. He was giving Betty some book titles and she was writing them down. Betty, noticing Ben's disapproving glance, made a point of not paying attention to Suzan. Suzan felt awkward and unwanted and she wondered if she should leave straight away. But then this would upset Ben and she would feel guilty about upsetting him. So she stood there in the middle of the room waiting. Finally Ben offered a gentle smile to Suzan and said to Betty: "That's it."

After Betty had left Ben tapped the edge of his bed and said: "Sit here my love."

She did as told.

"I was ordering some art books from Betty," he explained somewhat apologetically.

Suzan nodded to show that she didn't mind, then told him that she saw his cat again sitting grumpily in the yard of his studio.

"Maybe she is cross with me now," Ben frowned, "She won't dance for me when I return."

"Don't worry, I'll dance for you," Suzan said, grinning.

"Hmm," he grunted. Suzan's heart sank at his haughty expression and revolt flared up in her. He always frustrated her whenever sure of her love. He had done this during all the years they had been together.

But as if reading her thoughts, he grew suddenly light-hearted.

"Yesterday, Alan, my art dealer, phoned to tell me that my exhibition in Hon Kong was opening at that very moment," he told her. "And I could hear the nurse asking on the phone: 'Art dealer? Art dealer?' Then she came to me with the phone: 'An art dealer on the phone!' She said this as if it were a heroin dealer!" he grinned.

"After the phone call, I thought to myself, 'Here I am, in this poor hospital for dying people, while rich Chinese business men are talking about my paintings.' Isn't that funny?"

Suzan was glad about his success. But could it be the reason why he had looked down on her when she came in? Did he suddenly find her unworthy of a successful painter like himself?

20

Outside it was a day of boundless light. It was as though nature had stripped off the heavy clothes of winter. Suzan decided to go and see Irene who lived near the most southwesterly point. But as the bus stopped at Anthony's village, she got off impulsively and decided to call in at Anthony before walking to Irene's place.

She found Anthony sitting on the handmade wooden bench in the garden, the grass bordered by beds of freshly-pruned flowers.

"I won't stay. I'm going for a long walk today," she said.

"Come in." Anthony got up, stepping toward her, a broad smile expanding across his face. He led her to the house, "I'll make you a cup of tea."

As she followed him in, "I visited Ben yesterday," she said.

"How was he?"

"Rather pompous and arrogant."

"It means he is getting better." Anthony grinned.

As he poured hot water into two cups, standing in the kitchen he asked how far she was going to walk.

"As far as Irene's. Do you know her?"

"Yes. She was one of Ben's pupils, wasn't she?"

"Yes, long ago and one of his ex-lovers."

"I didn't want to mention that!" Anthony chuckled.

"Oh, I met most of his ex-lovers. Even Betty had been his lover long ago. "

"I couldn't do that with Betty," Anthony smirked handing her a mug.

"Well I think he had had a great number of girlfriends and lovers when he was young..." Suzan said, "Perhaps that shortened his life."

"That means I'll live to be a hundred." Anthony beamed.

They drank their tea in the garden, sitting on the bench. Suzan felt comfortable again in Anthony's company. And she wondered why he made her feel comfortable. Maybe because he was not pretentious, not pompous, not superior. He didn't seem to expect his companions to be very special. On the contrary, he seemed to accept them as they were. And perhaps he accepted himself also as he was. Not very special. Suzan staring at the well kept and picturesque garden became aware that without Anthony she would have felt horribly lonely in a time like this.

"Okay. I shall get on with my walk now," she smiled at him.

"Don't fall over the cliff while thinking too deep," he told her as he got up and gave her a warm hug.

"Look, I don't tap you on the shoulder any more," he joked.

Walking along the cliff she felt overwhelmed by the conflicting emotions inside her, then watching the view it occurred to her that the Cornish landscape was ambivalent too. It had somewhat an androgynous quality: the rocky cliffs masculine, but the moorland feminine; the cobalt blue colour masculine, but the green fields feminine. She remembered how Ben introduced her to Cornwall when she first came here ten years ago, taking her on his motorbike up and down the country, to the villages and deserted coves, along the country lanes and across the moor... He was eager to share his colossal enthusiasm for the natural beauty with her. "Look!" he would point, "Isn't that beautiful! Oh, we live in the most beautiful place in the world!"

Now gazing around, Suzan felt the memory of his enthusiasm will remain with her for the rest of her life.

As the string of houses of Lizard village appeared on the horizon, she searched for the footpath leading to Irene's house.

Irene, her lush fair hair glimmering in the sun, was working in the garden of her small whitewashed cottage. She laughed seeing Suzan, "I was thinking of you this morning!" she said.

"Oh yes, one of your telepathies!" Suzan said, knowing Irene's preoccupation with mysticism.

They had tea sitting on the grass in the sun. Blue-painted boats lingered in the tiny cove below.

"How is Ben?" Irene asked sadly.

Suzan said he would soon be back in his studio.

"I didn't go to the hospital, because I know he doesn't like spontaneous visits," Irene said.

"He didn't want to have visitors," Suzan explained.

"Oh, yes, he always set some rules!" Irene snapped laughing, then staring at the sea she went on, sadly, "And when you do not follow his rules, he makes you feel stupid! He was always critical of me. He made me feel inferior. But I was very sad when I heard about his illness, for he's really a character, he's unique. I don't know anybody like him. But I think Ben can't be close to anybody. I wonder whether he has any true friends."

"He has many, but also none," Suzan said. After a pause she added wistfully, "But..." she swallowed then looking up she said, "I did love him."

"So did I. Women like us need men who are different, who are exciting. And Ben is exciting. The world will be less exciting without him. I wrote him a letter and told him he can come here to convalescence. I thought if he can let go and relax, he might be cured. But I don't think he will do that."

Suzan was bewildered and shocked by Irene's gentle boldness but could say nothing.

Around eight that evening, Suzan went to Ben's studio.

"Come in," he called, "The door's unlocked."

He was in bed, listening to the radio.

"If you don't want to be disturbed…" Suzan said, seeing the hard expression on his face, "I just came to ask whether you need anything."

"Nothing," he shook his head, staring at the ceiling.

"Washing up? Cooking?"

"Betty gave me some pasta." He switched off the radio, "Everything's done. Sharon cleaned, and she did it so well."

He was implying that he was well looked after by other women.

Suzan, trying not to be offended, sat on the edge of his bed and said, "I can bring you lunch every day."

"No, thank you." He avoided her gaze as he grumbled, "I have too many visitors."

Suzan was hurt. When he was at the hospital he had given a special role: the only visitor. He perhaps needed a wife then, a wife visiting him in the hospital, like the other male patients around him. But now he was a noble bachelor whom people were eager to assist: cleaning, cooking, making the fire, building the new studio. They were useful people without any particular significance. He wanted to keep Suzan at a distance now because she had become once again too close to him, too significant. Perhaps he didn't want anybody to be too close to him because he was on his way to death.

"Jeanette gave me a kiss today," he suddenly said, trying to expel the sad mood. Jeanette was the fat woman working in the vegetable shop up the road. "She gave me two kisses," he expounded, showing with his two fingers.

Suzan smiled abstractedly, and sighed.

"I shall take a trip to Paris," she said, "If you don't really need my care."

He nodded, staring at the ceiling. And they remained silent for a few moments. Then she got up and made a few steps toward the window and then she stopped and faced him.

"I had a difficult time, too," she said, her voice slightly trembling. "I'm very upset about your illness. I try to look strong whenever I visit you, and cheer you up."

"I don't want to be cheered up," he frowned.

"But you didn't like me to be sad, either."

He remained indifferent, staring at the ceiling.

"All right," Suzan sighed. "I'll be off now. Can I do anything before I go?"

"Yes. Put some coal in the stove," he grumbled.

"Oh! You have a new stove!" she said in an attempt to be reconciled, pointing to the brand new cast iron stove with a window.

"Yes. It's very good," he said.

'Pity he won't need it for long,' Suzan thought to herself as she picked up the metal container.

"No! Not that! Take the bucket over there!"

She was shocked by his harsh and commanding voice. But she forced herself not to react. She looked around nervously to see where the bucket was. Since there was only one weak light on in the studio and he wouldn't like her to turn on other lights, she had difficulty finding the bucket. Suddenly a sense of revolt stirred inside her. 'Damn!' she thought. 'He's still tyrannical!'

Finally she put coal into the new cast-iron stove and as she was she leaving, she told him that she might go to Paris the next day.

There was silence. Then he spoke with a sudden touch of affection, "Enjoy your trip. Send me a postcard."

21

She returned from Paris two weeks later. And after leaving her luggage at Casa Mia, she rushed to his place, anxious to see him.

The wooden door was ajar.

He was on the bed, curled up. But hearing her voice, he straightened up with obvious difficulty. He was very elegantly dressed, red-striped shirt and bow tie. Although he had become threadlike, a noble appearance had come over him. He seemed determined not to be humiliated by the illness feeding on him.

"You look like Marcel Proust now," Suzan attempted to joke.

He held out his hand in contrived formality, but the expression on his lean and pale face betrayed excitement. When she hugged him, she heard his heart pounding within his shrunken warm chest.

He showed her to the green armchair and took his own usual seat.

"Help yourself," he pointed to the drinks.

As she was hesitating between the bottles, "Campari!" he said, "Have some Campari."

Her mind swiftly recaptured memories: sitting together outside a village café in Malta, a hot summer evening, sipping their Campari… Ben pointing to a woman with full buttocks, walking with her husband: "She has nice buttocks."

Pouring the Campari into two glasses, Suzan began to weep. She was crying for their past and for a future without him.

"I hope you don't mind me crying," she mumbled.

"Oh, I didn't know you were crying," he spoke softly.

She returned to her seat and put the glasses on the little hexagonal Victorian table.

"Don't be sad," he said in a whispering tone, "I am reconciled to death now."

That made her weep even more. Then she wiped her tears and her nose with a tissue and asked if he had had further treatment in the meantime.

"No." He shook his head, "I didn't want to have chemotherapy, because the doctor said it would only prolong my life for six months. I said it's not worth it. I want to die gracefully. I think any sensible person would do that."

She was again fascinated by his pride, his dignity. She raised her glass to him smiling fondly.

"How was your trip?" he asked.

"I stayed at my cousin's," she told him, "My poetry is published."

He gave a smile both sad and gentle, "Good. You deserve success."

She felt grateful, remembering how he always liked listening to her poems. She read them to him on Sunday evenings, sitting by the fire. And sometimes he read her poems from old poetry books, humorous poems, romantic poems... They felt so happy on such occasions then, so together, so compatible.

She did not tell him much about her trip. What was the point of telling a dying man about a trip? In the past, she used to tell him about funny incidents she had experienced during a trip, striving to excite him. Now she thought it would be unfair to excite him. She had not written to him while in Paris, and since he had no phone she could not phone him. But she had phoned Anthony twice to ask how Ben was. "Don't worry, we all are looking after him," Anthony had reassured her, "Ask him if he wants me to return," Suzan said. On her second call Anthony had told her to stay in Paris as long as she needed.

"And what about your recent exhibition?" Suzan asked after a sip from her Campari.

"Oh, it was a great success," Ben replied. "All the pictures are sold at very high prices."

"So you are rich and famous now."

"Umm," he nodded, then turned his face toward the window not pleased with she had just said.

'Damn! He might be thinking I expect money from him,' Suzan thought, observing him. But she was not expecting any money from him, not expecting any inheritance, even though she was hard up now, having not worked for a long time as supply teacher. Somehow she forbade herself to think about inheritance, as such a thought would make her feel bad about herself. But how could she assure him that she was not expecting any money from him?

"Marsha comes now every few days to see me," Ben offered, exuding contentment.

"Oh! Marsha?" Suzan was taken aback. She knew Marsha, and she knew about her lingering resentment against him since the accident she had had while coming to Tamarisk many years ago. The accident had left a big scar across Marsha's face. And she also knew that Marsha had not paid him back the money she had borrowed from him to buy a house in Penzance. Although he had tried to remain friends with Marsha after their separation some twenty years ago, Marsha turned down his offer of friendship. And now she was coming to see him now and then. Suzan remembered Ben telling her that he never had really loved Marsha, "She was good in bed and in the kitchen, but she was not stimulating, she was too middle-class." But now he sounded happy that Marsha was visiting him.

"Look, she brought me that shirt." He pointed to a blue workman's shirt on the back of a chair by the dining table.

Surely Marsha must have known that he wouldn't have much chance to wear it, Suzan thought, resentfully.

"Marsha has proved to be a good friend," Ben announced, looking out of the window, "She went to Tamarisk the other day with Andy, her older son. Andy might do some improvements there."

"Oh!" Suzan said, an expression of shock on her face and the idea hit her that Marsha could have a hidden agenda about Tamarisk, that she might want to take over Tamarisk after Ben's death. But what could she do to thwart Marsha's plans?

"Did you write new poems?" Ben asked to change the subject.

"Yes, a few," Suzan replied as she watched a skylark on the branch of a plum tree outside the window. "And did you paint new pictures?"

"No." Ben shook his head, "I feel very weak. It's such a nuisance! You spend most of your life learning your craft and then, when you have done so, someone switches off your life just like that. Is that God? What sort of God is it, if there is one? I don't believe in God! I'm more of a non-believer now than ever before."

Suzan did not react. He had never taken seriously the kind of spirituality she believed in. To him there was no other way. Either an absolute conviction or an absolute denial.

"Peter, the printer, was here the other day," he expounded, "I told him what I told you about God. Peter has a very wry sense of humour. Referring to my illness, he said, 'God gets jealous, that's why.'"

He gave a tired smile, looking at her. She was distant.

He told her how he had celebrated his birthday in the pub while she was away.

"When I was feeling tired and had retired to a corner, a beautiful girl came up and said, 'Ben, if I buy you a Jameson, would you slow dance with me?' The other men were very envious, because no girl came up to them offering whiskey and asking for a slow dance. So I had my whiskey and went onto the dance floor with the girl. We danced together beautifully. Then came a quick dance and I carried on. I did not leave the dance floor for two hours. It was the best birthday party I ever had." He looked at Suzan with a defiant smile.

Was this his way of getting revenge on her because she had gone away? But hadn't he always taken a cruel pleasure in flirting openly with other women, though he swore he did not go to bed with any of them. And now he was implying that even in the clutch of death, women were attracted to him and that he enjoyed their attention. But how could she reproach him? He always dismissed her reproaches. He behaved as if he was above all reproaches and judgments. He behaved like a king, And now how he had put himself on a kind of throne, too, reigning over all those remaining alive while he was dying. And he was determined to uphold his Epicurean philosophy until his last breath. He was still in competition with human destiny, with the futility of life. He wanted to have fun at all costs. Only a short period of life was left to him and he must make the best of it. He must take advantage of that treacherous life.

"I was worried about you," he offered with sudden tenderness. "I thought you might have been murdered in Paris."

She smiled remembering. Whenever she left him in the past, he said he feared she had been murdered. Maybe that was what he subconsciously wished to happen to her all along. His passion for her had always mingled with his wish to see her vanish. Perhaps he feared that his passion might consume him. So, one of them had to vanish, to be sacrificed. And now he was going to vanish and was perhaps paradoxically glad.

"I phoned Anthony to ask about you," Suzan said to imply that she did not forget him while in Paris.

He did not react to this. And staring into the distance, his face grew cold and rigid. Suzan wondered if he now suspected her having an affair with Anthony. But as if reading her thoughts and to shield himself against inappropriate feelings such as jealousy, he spoke in sudden amiability,

"I like Anthony. He comes here every few days to bring wood and coal and light the stove."

Hearing this, a doubt stirred inside Suzan. Anthony had never been really close to Ben. And he had strangely supported her in going to Paris and encouraged her to stay there as long as she wished. Did Anthony have some hidden agenda?

"The reason I did not write to you, is…" Suzan paused, feeling nervous under his stare. But then she decided to tell him what weighed on her heart. "You began treating me as one of your visitors and told me you didn't want any visitors."

"What's wrong with that?" he growled. "I can't handle them. I want to rest."

"But I'm not a visitor!" she raised her voice. "When I visited you in the cottage hospital and Betty was there, you sulked when you saw me…"

"For God's sake! It wasn't a garden party! I don't want to hear your criticisms any more! And I won't apologize for anything!"

Suzan trembled. How frightening he still could be!

"It's not a criticism…" she mumbled, "Just an explanation. You blamed me for not writing you from Paris… So I want you to know that it wasn't selfishness. I sensed you had started suspecting me. I visited you only when you wanted me to."

"That's correct, and so should the other visitors."

"I'm not one of your visitors!" She raised her voice again, "And I don't want to show you a false kindness and tolerate everything you do just because…" she broke off, clasping the arms of her armchair. Then, adopting a calmer tone, she said: "I want to treat you as an equal."

He turned his face away and his eyes rested on the sculpture on the shelf. It was Suzan's head. Suzan too stared at the sculpture he had done of her after their separation. He turned a smiling face to her then said, "I smoke marijuana every evening now. At eight o'clock I have my marijuana and my morphine. Then I go to bed and listen to the radio till I fall asleep."

"You always lived to a routine," Suzan gave a wistful smile.

He nodded somewhat sternly. After a moment of silence, he resumed, "I don't accept visitors in the evenings. I tell everybody not to visit me in the evenings. But you know what happened? The other night there was a bang on the door. I woke up, looked at my watch: quarter to eleven. 'Who's that?' I shouted. A mumbling little voice came from behind the door. I didn't recognize it. I thought somebody might be in trouble and need help. So I went to the door, half opened it and immediately a hand gripped the door. My first instinct was to shut it but I couldn't do that without smashing the hand. I recognized Maria. You know Maria, the alcoholic, the mad woman from Portlando. I said: 'I can't receive a visitor at this hour. What do you want?' 'I must talk to you! I must talk to you!' she moaned. 'Okay, five minutes,' I said. She burst into the room and fell to her knees, grabbing my legs: 'Please don't die! Please don't die! Promise you won't die!' Oh, I got so angry. I said, 'I'm not going to die. Get up and leave!' So I got her out, almost by force."

He paused and smiled remotely, "It's good to see you back."

"I missed you," Suzan said softly and looked toward the window to suppress tears.

"I didn't have any big relationship after ours," he expounded in a grave tone, "though women are still interested."

"You make them interested," Suzan faced him with a hint of a smile.

He chose to ignore this and, looking at the clock on the wall opposite, he said, "It's half past eight, time for my marijuana."

He rose and they hugged. His body was mere bones now. He disliked thin people, thin women, Suzan remembered. Now as she held him, she knew he was embarrassed by his own skinny body.

He wanted to walk with her to the wine shop to buy cigarettes. As they crossed the yard, he touched her arm and said, "Come I'll show you my orchard."

He led her through an alleyway to the land at the back of the building. He had planted the orchard as soon as he had moved into the barn. The young apple trees were now bearing their first leaves. Looking at the large garden, mowed lawn, a lush vegetable garden at the bottom, and in the distance the hilly landscape with the fields in different shades of green, 'The orchard would be his last gift to the town, to the world,' Suzan said to herself. Standing beside him and staring at the trees, "Do you want me to look after you?" Suzan asked softly.

"No, thank you," he said, "Sharon is looking after me. She's very nice."

"But she's silly and noisy," Suzan said vindictively.

"I have been with deep and intelligent women in the past," he grumbled. Then he led her out. Arriving at the wine shop he kissed her lightly on the cheek and asked like a little boy, "Shall we meet in the Fat Man café at half past ten tomorrow?"

22

The next morning, as she walked up the street, she saw him coming down. He looked frailer than ever. Overcome by compassion she rushed to him and threw her arms around him. But he remained distant and shot her a reprimanding glance.

"What's this?" He pointed to her beige suede jacket.

"It's genuine suede," Suzan said disconcertedly.

"But already screwed up," he spluttered.

"Oh, perfectionist! You never give up," she said, trying to take it easy.

"I can't stand, I must walk on," he grumbled, leaning on his stick. "I'm going to have my hair cut by the hairdresser above the café."

But once in the café his grumpiness subsided.

"You sit there," he said softly, pointing to their usual table by the window. "I have to go upstairs to have my hair cut."

He climbed the stairs leaning on his stick, his thin legs unsteady.

She sat and ordered coffee. After a few moments she saw him coming down the stairs.

"What happened?"

"Natasha is behind her schedule. So I have to wait." He sat, then waved to the girl behind the counter to order his espresso.

"Why didn't you like my jacket?" Suzan asked cautiously.

"I don't like that whole ensemble and I don't like your hair tied up like that," he demonstrated.

She took off her jacket and untied her hair, letting it fall over her shoulders.

"How do I look now?" She tilted her head playfully.

"Oh! you look better by the minute." Joining his hands, he mimed admiration.

Suzan, laughing, stretched out her hand to hit him.

His espresso arrived and he leaned back, unwinding.

"The day after Maria banged on my door at a quarter to eleven," he began to recount charmingly, "there was a knock again at about nine in the evening. I shrank, thinking that it must be that mad woman again. I went carefully to the door; opened it slightly and saw three old ladies standing on my doorstep. One of them said in a broad Yorkshire accent, 'Are you Ben Duncan?' I said, 'Yes.' 'I am your mother's cousin. We are looking for your mum and dad.' 'Then you must look for them up in heaven,' I said, pointing up, 'and I am going to join them there soon.' They looked at me terrified, as if they saw a ghost."

He chuckled with these last words, although his eyes remained sad. Then he turned his face to the female voice calling him from the staircase. It was his hairdresser signalling. He got up, laying a hand on Suzan's arm as he passed her seat, a gleam of affection in his eyes; an apology for having scolded her badly on the street.

Suzan gave him a reassuring smile. Then, waiting for him, she wondered whether she should run home and change, put on something he would like. But thinking it would exasperate him even more if he didn't see her when he came down, she waited.

When he returned to the table, his hair was trimmed, a youthful fringe on his forehead,

"Wow!" she cheered. "You've got the best hairstyle in town!"

"Hmm," he said, pouting, and sat down. Suzan told him that she had nearly run home to change her clothes.

"You have such an effect on me," she said, "and you still manipulate me."

"I don't manipulate you." He gave her an offended look, then asked her if she would like another coffee.

When he went to the counter to pay, Suzan observed him from behind. So thin and weak, yet still so charming, so charming, with his cloth cap and the new workman's shirt Marsha had bought for him.

They left the café. She walked behind him, letting him determine their pace. He suggested they go to the jumble sale at the Guild Hall. They used to visit the place on Saturdays, buying old books, jugs or glasses.

A heavy green velvet curtain spread out on a table at the entrance caught Suzan's eye, distracting her from the disquieting recollection.

"Oh, I can buy it and make a tablecloth from it," she pointed.

"You can have mine after I am gone," he said flatly.

"Don't say that," she mumbled.

They left the jumble sale without buying anything. He, who had always been so eager to buy antique objects, was no longer interested. On their way to his studio he wanted to sit on a bench on the pavement, occupied mostly by hippies and travellers in town. But the bench was now occupied by two elderly men dressed in grey bomber jackets campaigning for Cancer Research, an improvised table with handmade puppets on it placed in front of them. Ben grumbled, trying to make room for Suzan and himself, "This bench is for people to sit on and socialize, not for such campaigns."

The men ignored him.

"The other day, two fellows from the British Legion were collecting money here for the Lion's Club," he told her, "I got so angry. John, the traveller, was sitting on the steps of the shop behind. I told him to sit on the bench with me. 'This bench is not for your bloody British Legion, or your bloody Lion's Club, it is for the people of this town!' I told the men."

Suzan could not suppress her giggles and said in a whispering tone, "Now you can offend anyone and any institution you like. You can even commit any crime you like, they won't put you in jail."

Startled and dismayed by the word 'crime', he merely nodded. Then he told her he wanted to buy lamb burgers spiced with mint.

"Do you want some burgers for your lunch too?" he asked her.

"No thanks. I don't eat meat, remember?"

He had never really acknowledged that she was vegetarian. And when they were together, he kept buying huge pieces of lamb or beef to roast for their Sunday lunch.

As they walked on towards his place, he ahead of her, the sight of his white and wrinkled neck caught her eyes. She felt the kind of affection one would feel for one's own sick child.

He bent to pick a flower from the pavement, a bright purple one apparently dropped by a passer-by, and with great difficulty placed it in his breast pocket, next to the handkerchief. But after a moment the flower fell out. Suzan picked it up and replaced it in his breast pocket. They smiled simultaneously.

Having arrived in the studio, he asked her if she would fry the burgers for him. He would have them later, around five, warming them up. Suzan agreed. He went to the basement to make some phone calls. That was where he stored his paintings and had his wardrobe, his desk and a newly installed telephone, following Linda's suggestion.

"Why don't you keep the phone by your bedside?" Suzan asked.

"The phone should be where I do my paperwork, at my desk," he replied sternly.

On Monday, passing the café, Suzan saw Ben sitting with Alan, his art dealer. Ben waved enthusiastically, beckoning her to come in, and when she did so, he went to fetch a chair for her. Nobody could beat him in good manners, even now, thought Suzan. The empty plates smeared with tomato sauce showed that he and the dealer had had an English breakfast.

But soon after Suzan sat, Ben said they had been in the café for two hours, and he was feeling very tired.

"Do you mind if I go? Alan can stay for a while so you can talk. I can go by myself."

"Are you sure?" Suzan was worried.

"Yes," he replied. Then he laid a hand on her shoulder, as he got up. "Do you have an answering machine?" he asked her.

"Yes."

"I have one too. Now our answering machines can talk to each other." He winked.

He took a ten pound note out of his pocket and handed it to Alan. "That should cover all this."

Alan took the money and smiled, "Thanks, Ben."

Ben walked out. Alan and Suzan followed him with their eyes. Then Alan said, "He is a brave man."

"Yes." Suzan nodded, a lump in her throat.

"I arrived yesterday and we had a wonderful evening," Alan expounded. "He sent Sharon to buy new potatoes and lamb chops, and he cooked, although I didn't want him to. 'I can take you out for dinner,' I said, 'No, no, I'll cook,' he insisted. But then, in the middle of the meal, he felt tired and had to lie down. It's so sad. How long, do you think?"

"Not long..." she said, looking away, fighting back tears again, "He has given up. He doesn't want to struggle any more."

"It must be very difficult for you."

"Yes. It is. Especially in these circumstances. If we were together it could have been easier... Now I don't know how to behave. We have been very close, you know."

"Yes, I know. He speaks very fondly of you."

"Does he?"

"Yes. I think you have been the most significant person in his life."

She lowered her face.

"I'm glad I did come down," Alan resumed with a sad smile. "He talks in a very matter-of-fact manner of his imminent death. I'll try to make him fully recognized, upheld. People should not forget him."

"Yes. You must do your best. He has been very honest in his art."

"And his portraits of you are the best part of his work. You too will be remembered."

Suzan smiled in order not to cry.

23

Primroses and daffodils were flourishing, but the air was still chilly and the sky close and grey. Suzan made a big bunch of them, thinking Ben might be motivated to do some colour drawings. He had done such drawings in the past and dedicated to her scribbling on them, 'I love you'. Oh, he was so generous with such words and made her feel so valuable, so loved. She also took his enthusiasm and passion for granted most of the time and chose not to reciprocate fearing his other self, the destructive self lurking within him. But now she wanted to give him generously her love, her affection and thus perhaps make him live longer. She would try to inspire him to paint again and live longer. She would give him Beta carotene and high doses of vitamin C and a spoon of honey mixed with nettle seeds every day.

With this in mind she collected nettles, went to the pharmacy to buy supplements and returning home she changed, putting on her white linen blouse, rose coloured long skirt and her straw hat. Examining herself in the mirror, she decided he would like to see her like that and taking the bunch of flowers she went to his studio.

Crossing the yard, she heard Sharon's loud laughter, and climbing the steps she caught a glimpse of her, standing in front of the sink in tight black shorts, her red frizzy hair hiding her face. She called out to Ben and waited. Sharon came to the door. "Oh! come in!" She treated her like a visitor, and returned to her washing up.

Ben looked very pale in the bright morning light, sitting on his white armchair.

"You look as if you are going to a garden party," he teased her with a faint smile.

She put the flowers in a jug.

"They're nice," he said, then pointed to the top shelf where the sculptures stood. "Put them over there." Suzan did as she was told and sitting on the armchair opposite him, she said, "I also bought vitamins for you."

He gave her a painful look, as if to say, 'it's not worth it.' Then he suggested they go to the café while Sharon cleaned the studio.

"We won't go anywhere unless you take those vitamins," Suzan raised her index finger in mock authority.

"Okay," he murmured, somewhat pleased with her authority, "Give me vitamins."

After taking the vitamins he looked up at her, like an obedient child, "Can we go to the Fat Man café?"

"Yes," Suzan smiled, "Let's."

He raised his hand to Sharon as he walked out followed by Suzan, "See you later, Sharon."

He stood on the doorstep and beaming he spread out his hand: "Oh, look it's summer!"

On their way to the café it occurred to Suzan that he was no longer looking at attractive women in summer clothes as he used to do in the old days. He had lost interest in women's bodies, perhaps because his own body did not exist any longer.

In the café he sat on his usual seat by the window, the sun cast a sharp pool of light upon him, emphasising the hollowness and pallor of his face. Suzan, eager to inspire him, told him about a film she had seen: a young student trying to keep a suicidal ex-colonel alive. But the obvious implication of her effort left Ben cold. Suzan broke off, seeing him contort his face.

"Are you bored?"

"I feel tired and very hot." He gave her a sour look, which made her feel guilty.

"Take off your waistcoat," she said.

"I can't!" he grumbled. "I have my wallet and some papers in my pocket."

"I can keep them in my handbag for you."

He finally agreed. In the past he wouldn't have agreed.

As he tried to slip out of the felt waistcoat, she got up to help him. She gently held his thin weak arms. How robust and vibrant these arms used to be! She would miss his embrace.

She told him about her intention to prolong his life with high doses of vitamins and herbs. One woman who had cancer lived three years longer than the doctors expected with the help of those vitamins.

"But I don't want to live three more years," he grumbled, "I can't paint any more. What's the point of living any longer?"

"You can do some drawings, colour drawings of flowers," Suzan bent towards him, as if begging him for collaboration.

"I can only do what I want to do," he grumbled.

He had never compromised his art. He never cheated in painting, thought Suzan, a wave of admiration inside her.

After a moment she saw him greet a fat blonde woman passing by.

"My nurse," he told Suzan. "One of the Macmillan nurses. Do you know what Macmillan nurses do?"

"No."

"They attend dying people," he said in an unsentimental voice.

Suzan, wishing to go along with his light-hearted attitude, smiled: "She is attractive, your type."

"Yes very," he nodded. "When they phoned and asked me whether I wanted to have a particular nurse, I said, 'Yes, the most attractive one.' Then they sent me this one and I like her very much."

"Good." Suzan smiled again.

He said that he was expecting a man who wanted to write a book about him and that he planned to offer him salad Niçoise and cheese for lunch.

"I can make the salad," Suzan offered.

"That'd be nice."

They went to the bakery together to buy white rolls, then to the delicatessen shop to buy cheese, black olives and anchovies. When they arrived at the studio Sharon was leaving.

"It was nice seeing you, Suzan." Sharon gave a contrived smile.

"See you soon, Sharon," Suzan replied, trying to forget the scene in the supermarket.

She gave Ben a spoon of nettle seeds mixed with honey and some vitamins. He complied and went to lie down. She set out to prepare the salad. As she was washing the lettuce leaves, she heard him say, "Jane is coming on Friday. She will be here for two days and will stay at Tamarisk."

Suzan was silent, exercising self-control and struggling to quell the rush of revolt inside her. She had never met Jane but had seen her photographs and letters dated some twenty years ago and kept in the chest of drawers at Tamarisk. She looked attractive on her photographs, she looked like a college girl determined to have a good time.

"I didn't invite her," Ben went on, suspicious of Suzan's silence, "She invited herself. She became a Buddhist you know." He was saying this perhaps to prevent Suzan's jealousy, knowing her interest in Buddhism.

"Which salad bowl and which plates?" Suzan asked, her voice slightly coarse.

"What?" He turned his face to her, widening his eyes.

"Which bowl, which plates shall I use?" Suzan pointed to the wooden shelf where plates were kept.

"Chinese porcelain," he replied with a slight grimace, frustrated by her lack of reaction about Jane's visit. "They are in the cupboard."

In the silence that followed Suzan set the table.

"Thank you." His voice was soft again.

She went to him and kissed him on both cheeks.

"Don't forget to take your vitamins tomorrow morning."

He nodded in childlike obedience.

24

Suzan did not go to see Ben for the next three days and wrestled with the somewhat absurd jealousy gnawing at her. Not only was she disturbed by Jane's visit, whose photographs she had seen in a drawer at Tamarisk, but also by the fact that she was staying at Tamarisk. The house where Ben and herself had had their happiest time and where before her, he had entertained his girlfriends, Jane included. She was afraid of meeting Jane, whom she imagined to be more beautiful than she herself and also because she feared she might not control her feelings of jealousy.

Yet on the third day, passing by the studio, on her way to do shopping, she saw her. A fair woman in her early forties, her hair cut short, crossing the yard. She was wearing khaki shorts and a white linen blouse and exuded a well rooted sophistication. Suzan found herself walking towards her, as though against her will.

They exchanged glances of uncertain recognition.

"Are you Jane?" Suzan asked, coming nearer. She was glad that Jane was not as beautiful as on her photographs taken long ago. She had a tanned, lean face, green eyes, with eyelids drooping upon them and a large chin which disturbed the proportion of her face.

"Yes." Jane smiled with a sad curiosity, "And you are Suzan."

They shook hands. A moment of suspense followed. They expected questions from one another, but then settled to a silent acceptance.

"Is Ben upstairs?" Suzan asked.

"Yes, he is," Jane replied gently.

"Are you staying at Tamarisk?"

"I stayed there my first night but it was too damp. Now I'm staying here, in the new studio. But I shall go to Tamarisk this afternoon again. Oh, I love Tamarisk!" Jane's eyes sparkled with passion as she said that and Suzan, with a pang at revolt inside her, looked away.

"See you later," she forced a smile and walked towards the wooden steps.

Ben, sitting on his chair, beamed seeing Suzan and raised his hand:

"Oh hello! I missed you! Why didn't you call in?"

Suzan said nothing.

"Help yourself to a glass of sherry."

She did so and sat on the chair opposite him.

"How are you today?" she asked, rather formal.

"I have eaten a lot of a sheep," he announced gleefully.

"Sheep? You mean lamb?"

"Yes, Jane brought a huge piece of sheep from her farm. Her husband is a farmer, you see. She cooked a wonderful stew yesterday, all with organic vegetables. I enjoyed it very much."

Suzan hated this provocation.

But Ben went on, "Today we are going to have dinner at Betty's. Betty wants to see Jane. They used to be good friends…"

"I see…" Suzan looked away. Another stab at revenge by Betty, Suzan thought. Betty still ignored her. As she was about to voice her dismay, she was confronted with Ben's reproachful stare as if to say that she had no right to be critical because he was a dying man.

Jane burst in cheerfully and asked Suzan if she would like a cup of coffee.

"No, thanks," Suzan mumbled, trying to appear friendly.

Jane stood in front of the sink, washing the dishes.

"I'm using your sock, because the sponge here is dirty," she said to Ben holding a blue sock up playfully.

"Oh! My favourite socks! They're Italian!" Ben moaned by way of a joke.

"Okay, okay. Don't worry," Jane laughed. "I'll wash them afterwards and you'll be able to wear them."

Suzan felt the urge to leave.

"Why are you going?" Ben pouted.

"I have things to do." Suzan rose, forcing a smile.

Supporting himself on the arms of his chair, he rose, too, and stood in front of her. Then he put his hand gently on her shoulder, looked fondly and deeply in the eyes and kissed her tenderly on the lips. This romantic manifestation wiped away Suzan's anger and restored her. Glancing at Jane, she saw her lower her face toward the sink.

"It was nice meeting you, Jane," Suzan said, walking to the door.

"Nice meeting you too. I hope we'll meet again," Jane turned her face to Suzan and smiled.

"Come whenever you like, my love," Ben addressed Suzan, and, standing in the middle of the room, he waved to her through the open door until she turned round the corner.

25

The next morning he phoned her to ask if she would like to come over. Jane had already left.

"Yes. I'll be there in about an hour," Suzan said eagerly.

The door was open and he was lying in bed.

"It's nice to lie here and think," he said when she sat on the edge of his bed. She stroke his face.

He looked at her ambiguously, perhaps craving her touch and yet afraid of anything which might excite him and make it even more difficult for him to surrender to the approaching death.

Suzan continued to stroke his forehead, his hair, then she bent toward him and said, "I want to be buried with you."

He looked bewildered; then, as if to block the flood of emotions, he said flatly: "But you must buy your plot beforehand."

"I'll do that," she smiled sadly.

"And you must pay for it. It costs six hundred pounds."

"Yes, I'll pay for it. Do you want me to be buried with you?"

"Yes," he whispered, looking at the ceiling.

"We'll not quarrel there," she tried to be mischievous. His expression froze; he was not pleased.

Regretting her clumsy joke, she said hastily: "Shall I cook something you like?"

"No, thank you. Jane left me some ravioli. I shall warm it up later. Jane was very sensitive and very generous."

Here, we go, Suzan thought, the old game of his, playing women against each other. Observing his frail body as he struggled to get up, she admitted the absurdity of her jealousy and said dryly, "Yes, she is very nice."

She went to the inbuilt kitchen to make herbal tea.

"Which cup do you fancy? Big or small?"

"Big," he said. "The Georgian cup. The one used by the King."

"Okay, my highness," she grinned. She gave him tea in a pink floral antique cup, assuming it was the Georgian cup.

"No," he said, "this is pre-Georgian, but it's all right, I'll have the pre-Georgian cup, you can have the Georgian one."

They grinned simultaneously. They had their tea, sitting by the window.

"Oh, I felt terrible this morning," he told her. "The nurses did horrible things to me." He contorted his face in disgust.

"What sorts of things?"

"They washed my bowels."

"With pills?"

"No, they stuck something in my bottom." He frowned childishly. "But they were very nice, the nurses. Very nice people. One man, one woman. Very correct and competent, old-fashioned. I said to them, 'What a funny job you've got, going around on Saturday mornings sticking things into gentlemen's bottoms.'"

That night she woke by his call. He was in panic because he couldn't get through on the phone to Gisela Meyer and her husband in Worpswede whom he expected in two days' time.

"Oh! I hate this telephone! I don't need it. I'll smash it, throw it away!" His weak voice vibrated with wild anger.

Suzan asked if he would like her to phone Gisela and ask her to call him back.

"No! Then I'll be restless waiting for her call."

"Do you want me to come over and help you to call?"

"No. I don't want to see anybody right now!"

"All right. Is there anything I can do? Hold on. Why don't you phone directory inquiries and check the number, then phone the operator and ask her to connect you?"

"Oh! It's too complicated! Digitals! Why did I buy this horrible, modern thing! I paid one hundred and fifty pounds for it! It was Linda's idea! It just spoils my life. Today I was feeling physically and mentally healthy and now I have dyslexia. I can't write down the number of directory inquiries."

"Don't panic. Don't panic," Suzan spoke in a motherly tone, "Relax."

The next morning, when she went to see him, he told her that he decided not to use the telephone any more. However, he had managed to get through to the Meyers the previous night. Although he had tried to discourage them, they were determined to come.

Suzan washed up the dirty glasses and plates piled up in the sink by visitors the day before. Sharon had a day off. When she was finished with the washing up, she asked him if she could get him something to eat.

He wanted a sandwich: "Square, white bread with only Cheddar cheese in it."

But Suzan could not buy a square sandwich in the bakery because they had sold out, so she bought a white bap filled with Cheddar cheese. But was worried that Ben being so set on his 'square sandwich with cheddar cheese' wouldn't eat it.

But luckily he compromised and ate the bap.

"You have become like the little boy they talked about on the radio the other day," Suzan said, "The boy who refused to eat anything but jam sandwiches for three years."

"Oh, yes, I heard the programme. Then there was a parody on it. Did you listen to that too?"

"No."

He told her that in the parody the boy's mother kept asking him what he would like to eat and each time the boy demanded a different kind of jam. Then suddenly he surprised his mother saying 'Roast beef' and the mother said

'I'll get you jam'. So it wasn't jam, it was poverty," Ben concluded.

That afternoon when she knocked on his door no answer came. She went in and found him sleeping, his lips slightly parted. The only sign that he was alive was the slight movement of his belly as he breathed. She shuddered, thinking that one day she would come in and find him dead.

He opened his eyes and his face lit up seeing her at his bedside.

"Can we have some tea?" he asked immediately.

"Yes. We shall have tea." She stroked his forehead. Then helped him get up and, holding him by the waist, and led him to his armchair.

"I feel very tired today," he moaned, "And yesterday, when I went to buy a meat pie, I nearly asked an elderly lady, 'Excuse me, could you carry me to my place please?'"

Suzan smiled, at once sad and amused.

As they sat together having tea, there was a knock at the door.

"Come in," Ben called.

And there she was: Tracy, looking striking in her long purple velvet skirt and tight black jacket, her bushy auburn hair tied loosely on top of her head, her fine face sparkling with youth and health. Seeing her, Ben beamed but then turned an inquisitive gaze to Suzan. Suzan glared at him.

"I'm going to sleep soon," Ben told Tracy gently yet firmly.

But Tracy ignored him. She came and stood in the middle of the room and started to talk eagerly, ignoring his reluctance. She talked about an accident that had occurred on the motorway, she talked about the harvest festival in the village of Snake Cliff, about the carnival and the procession, about the old clothes she had bought at the flee market...

"Take a seat," said Ben breaking her avalanche of speech.

Suzan got up and as she walked to the kitchen she asked Tracy: "Fancy a cup of tea?"

Tracy sat at the dining table while Suzan made tea for her. She told Ben that she had left her parents' home a week ago.

"Where do you live now?" Ben asked.

"With an old lady in town. Is anyone living at Tamarisk?"

"I don't know what I am going to do with Tamarisk." Ben grunted staring into the distance. Suzan returned to her seat. An uneasy silence fell upon the room.

Tracy broke the silence: "Do you need hash, Ben? I have some with me."

Ben, slightly startled by the blatant offer, spoke carefully: "Thank you, not today; I'll let you know."

Tracy finished her tea and put the cup on the table, then she started another jabber. She said she had been to Sheffield recently, but did not much like it there.

"If you don't know the town you can't enjoy it," said Ben, "But if I took you and showed you the parts of the town worth seeing, you would have a different impression."

"I'm sure I would!" Tracy smiled charmingly.

"I've been to Sheffield, three years ago," Suzan chimed in.

Ben then told Tracy how Suzan had phoned him from Sheffield.

"We had a row previously. Then Suzan phoned me and said, 'Guess where I am.' I said, 'I don't give a damn where you are, madam.'"

Suzan glared at him. What he had just said was not true. When she phoned him from Sheffield, he told her, "We must go there together one day." But now he was lying to entertain Tracy at Suzan's expense.

Finally succumbing to tiredness, he said, "Why don't you two go to the garden and watch the sun set?"

But Tracy decided to leave. And Suzan washed the cups while he retired to bed.

Then she, too, left, unable to utter any reproach.

But the next morning when she went to give him his pills, she flared up.

"I'm angry! That girl wants to squat at Tamarisk and settle down there!"

"I don't think so," Ben mumbled, avoiding her gaze.

"But you have not refused her request. Not firmly, not clearly. And besides, you ridiculed me to entertain her! Then what is worse, you are buying hash from her!"

Ben remained silent and gave her an oddly sympathetic look. He seemed pleased that she shouted at him, just like in the old days and ignored his illness.

"You treat me as if I am a silly and emotional woman," Suzan went on, gesticulating, walking up and down, "You may be thinking I'm expecting something from you. Well, I'm not! Don't give me anything! Anything! And don't misinterpret my affection. All I feel for you now is compassion, nothing else!"

He kept staring at the ceiling and when she stopped shouting and walked to the window, he said rather tenderly, "Shall we have some tea now?"

Suzan turned round, a bewildered smile across her flushed face, as she recognised his old trick. He always retreated in front of her firm revolt and ridiculed her anger by simply coming up with an offer.

"All right. We shall have some tea." She was suddenly embarrassed by her own outburst of anger. "But you must take your vitamins first. You might live two more years if you take enough vitamins."

"But I don't want to live two more years," he pouted.

"If you don't want to live, then I won't give you the vitamins." She was brisk again.

"Okay, give me my vitamins."

She gave him tea and vitamins. She sat on the edge of his bed and they drank their tea quietly.

As she was leaving she kissed him on the cheek.

"Keep calling in, my love," he whispered.

26

When Suzan came in the next morning, she found him standing in the middle of the room, in his underwear, white cotton shorts and short-sleeved top, which displayed his thread-like, pale limbs.

"I thought the Germans arrived," he murmured, "Gisela and Reinhard are to arrive this morning."

"Are they coming today? Shall I then tidy up here before they come?"

"That would be nice." He staggered back to bed.

While she was washing up, a white Mercedes stopped outside. After a few minutes Gisela walked in cheerfully – "Hello! Hello!" Fit and vigorous like an athlete, despite her cropped grey hair – a big bunch of flowers in her hand she was followed by Reinhard who, with his bald head and long, frizzy ginger beard looked like a priest.

After greeting Suzan rather casually, Gisela rushed to Ben's bed, kissed him on both cheeks and helped him spryly to sit up, supporting his back with two cushions. Then, crossing the room with her mercurial gait, she went to the dining table, removed the wilting flowers from the vase and replaced them with the fresh ones she had brought. Then she wiped the table with the sponge.

She returned to Ben's bedside, followed by Reinhard. They both sat on the edge of his bed and started telling him about their journey in great details. How they had left Worpswede, how everybody in the village sent him their love, how they stopped in London and how they had stayed at a B&B in Okehampton, etc, etc...

"We couldn't afford to stay in a hotel, we have no money," Reinhard finally said which made Gisela frown at him.

She asked Ben whether he was able to go out.

"I haven't been out in the last few days," Ben said. "Our café has been closed, but now they've reopened it. He swivelled his head towards Suzan and said, "We must go there again, my love."

Gisela chimed in: "We'll go there, Ben! We'll also go to Tamarisk. I and Reinhard can stay there can't we?"

Hearing that, Suzan shivered and it occurred to her that Tamarisk had become an object of desire for all those who came to see him on his death bed. Perhaps each of them dreamed of taking over Tamarisk. Suzan was overcome by the desire to fight for Tamarisk. For Tamarisk meant Ben, it meant his enthusiasm, his passion, his art. Absorbed by the frenzy of his terminal illness and by their renewed relationship, she had pushed away any thought about inheritance and about who would be the beneficiary of his estate. But now as she watched Gisela and Reinhard talk frantically to him, bent over him, as though wanting to take him away from the woman who had once possessed him and perhaps brought him to his doom. Suzan remembered how Gisela had ignored her during all those years. In Worpswede whenever she asked Ben over to their house for a meal, she excluded Suzan. Was that jealousy? Perhaps Gisela, rigidly and eternally settled within her matrimonial and motherly role, found an imaginary lover in Ben.

She now appeared so energetic, so eager in their desire to own him on his death bed that Suzan had to retreat, at least for the time being. She asked them if they would like to have tea.

"That would be nice," Gisela replied robustly.

Suzan made tea, gave everybody a cup, and took her leave.

"Come whenever you fee like it, my love. Don't feel excluded," Ben offered with emphatic tenderness in an attempt perhaps to fool Gisela and Reinhard and show them his priority.

Suzan was surprised to find Gisela and Reinhard on her doorstep the next morning. Gisela knew the house. She and Reinhard and their two children had stayed there a few times. It was before Suzan had entered Ben's life.

As soon as she came in Gisela started to examine the house, eager to remember it as it had been when Ben's parents lived in there. Her connection to the house gave her somehow another excuse to ascertain her own significance in Ben's life and treat Suzan as though she were an intruder, a newcomer.

While having coffee in the kitchen, she pointed to the pine kitchen table.

"That's a nice table! I would like that in my home."

Suzan ignored the implication, although it crossed her mind again that the motive of their trip may be other than just to say goodbye to their dying friend.

Gisela told Suzan that they were frustrated of having to look for alternative accommodation, because Ben did not offer them to stay at Tamarisk after all, saying that Andy, Marsha's older son, was there making some improvements.

"We love that house so much you know," said Gisela, "It became like our second home; we came to stay there every summer; it was before you and Ben met. We often helped him with the garden, with housework. We painted the walls, we cooked."

"Oh we have done so much for him," Reinhard chimed in emphatically. "He was very poor when we met him. And once, in Worpswede, he came to us and said he had no money to buy food. He was starving. So we gave him money."

Suzan was shocked by that revelation. It felt like a betrayal. And what did they want from her, Suzan wondered. They had demonstratively ignored her all along, including the day before, and now they seemed to seek an ally in her, knowing Suzan's frustration with their unfaithful friend.

"Oh, yes, we really supported him," Gisela said, "We once said to him 'We won't let you fall into the gutter, Ben.'"

"Yes, yes," Reinhard nodded earnestly, supporting his wife.

"Sorry, I've got things to do," Suzan finally said, rising.

"Of course," Gisela took no offence. "But hopefully we will have more time to talk later. And we will call on you whenever we are in Cornwall. We come to Cornwall every year."

When Suzan went to see Ben, she found Gisela and Reinhard in the basement, itemizing Ben's paintings.

"Look at these!" Reinhard uttered with a gleam of greed in his eyes, "They are all art!"

Who will benefit from the treasure the artist will leave behind? This was apparently the question that preoccupied them more overtly than the others. How tempting it was, to have an inheritance from an artist, who had no family and no wife. Probably each of them thought that if they didn't do it, someone else would.

27

In the Godolph Club that evening Lisa told Suzan that Sharon was known by many in town as a shoplifter.

"She hopes to rip Ben off and that is why she works for him," Lisa said, her sly green eyes twinkling. "And Sharon herself told me Ben had flirted with her, before he was taken ill," Lisa continued, absorbed by the thrill she created. "He had invited her out for dinner. He had even invited her to go to London with him."

Although she was aware of Lisa's love for drama and scandals, Suzan was shocked. My God, how could he be so mindless, how could he imagine spending time with Sharon, who had nothing to offer him other than housework and perhaps sex? Was that also an attempt to wipe out the wreckage of love left inside him after their split?

The following morning she bought two croissants from the small bakery opposite the delicatessen shop and went to his studio. She found Gisela dressing Ben on his bed. Seeing Suzan, his face lit up with a weary smile, although anguish lingered in his lovely candid eyes. And this immediately touched and disarmed Suzan. She was overcome by the desire to reassure him, but she refrained.

He tapped the edge of the bed wanting Suzan to sit beside him. And Gisela and Reinhard went to sit at the dining table for breakfast.

"Oh, Betty came again yesterday," Ben moaned. "Betty keeps coming every day, telling me she was just shopping in town. I told her, 'I don't like people visiting me every day just because I am ill.'" He broke off, seeing Sharon come in.

Sharon was dressed like a schoolgirl in a gym class, in black Lycra shorts and a black sleeveless Lycra top. As she set out hastily to change Ben's bed sheet, Suzan had no choice but sit at the table with Gisela and Reinhard.

Gisela told Sharon to come after breakfast the next time.

"I can't!" Sharon snapped.

Then she went over to Ben, who stood near the bed waiting for Sharon to finish. Her back turned to the others in the room, she took his face in both hands and kissed him on the lips. Then she whispered something into his ear. He smiled, somewhat shyly. Sharon kissed him again, well aware of being observed by the others.

Having put Ben in bed and covered him carefully with the freshly dressed duvet, Sharon left, striding dynamically across the room, hardly acknowledging the three onlookers. Suzan waited until Gisela and Reinhard went out. Then she sat on the edge of Ben's bed again and said she wanted a quiet word with him. He frowned, foreseeing the topic. Suzan, trying to be tactful, told him the rumours about Sharon's delinquent nature, her shoplifting and warned him that the woman might have hidden agenda.

"I'm not as foolish as you think," he grunted, looking away. "But I don't want to hurt people."

"What about hurting me? You have hurt me enough." Suzan snapped.

He gave her a startled and offended look.

"But…" Suzan's expression turned softer, "I am prepared to look after you until the end. And I want us to be reconciled. Truly reconciled." She paused, looked away, then spoke firmly: "But I don't want this woman to be around any longer."

"I can't make this choice." He shot her a sharp glance.

"But she is manipulative and—"

"Nobody is a hero," he interrupted her. "We have to tolerate the minor villains."

"Oh yes, tolerance!" Suzan was cynical. "Lately you've been intolerant even of my clothes. Now you're talking about tolerance! I have had enough of your double standards! Good bye." And so she left.

Walking down the street, she trembled with rage. Suddenly all the resentment she had been trying to suppress burst to the surface, eliminating all other considerations. She reminded herself that he had always ignored her feelings and opinions. Yet he managed to charm her over and over again, disarming her, enjoying his own victory and secretly despising her for forgiving him. Now, at the most inappropriate time, the time when he was most defenceless, she decided not to forgive him. She would not forgive him because forgiveness would drain not only her rekindled love for him, but her right for revenge. This was her last chance not to lose her love and self-defence at the same time.

Now she wanted to strike back before he went. She wanted to take the last decision, thus opposing all the decisions previously taken by him. This was her last chance to prove him wrong, to break up his game. She would now offer him the last chance to step back, the last chance to prove his respect to her, his respect for women, for womanhood, for he never really had any. He always believed he could manipulate all of them. Now Suzan would fight back. To do that, she must have the courage to appear to be a cruel woman taking her revenge on a dying man and maintain her anger till her anger went through him and led him to admit his mistake, led him to transform himself before he left his worldly existence. Her anger would cleanse her wounds, cleanse her current compromise and thwart his stubborn attempt to gloss over the injustice of the past. Once this last fight is fought, a true and genuine reconciliation would take place between them, Suzan thought. But now she must stand her ground.

The next morning, Gisela came to Suzan's as a messenger. Ben had said that the arrangement with Sharon could not be changed. But they would arrange things so that the two women, Sharon and Suzan, did not meet.

"But between us," Gisela confided as they sat in the kitchen over coffee, "we are glad that you warned Ben. We know that woman has bad intentions. But now please be generous; Ben said he enjoys your company."

"No," Suzan snapped, "I will not be generous any more. I gave him everything I had, my heart, my body, my mind. More generosity would mean giving up myself and my feelings for him."

Gisela nodded implying she understands, then said, "But thank you again," she said, "It was good you were the one who warned him about Sharon, so before leaving, we can organise everything and make it safe for him. We put the money he had left on the shelf into the bank. It was quite a large amount…"

She stared at Suzan, expecting her to ask 'how much?'

Suzan did not ask.

28

By a turn of destiny, a letter came from her publisher the next day asking her to come for the book launch. Suzan, eager to gain some distance, went to tell Ben about her plan to take another trip to Paris. He said, "It's better if you travel sooner so that I'm still around when you come back." Suzan told him that she would not stay in Paris longer than a week. While they were discussing this, Betty came in, bringing his supper. Betty had insisted on giving him supper at seven every evening since the departure of Gisela and Reinhard, even though Suzan had suggested she did it herself. Betty told Suzan that it was a pleasure to bring Ben his supper every evening. So there was no way Suzan could reverse Betty's decision.

"Of course you should go to Paris," said Betty.

At nine on Sunday morning, Suzan knocked at Ben's door.

"I can't open it!" she heard him grumble, struggling with the lock behind the door.

"Leave it, leave it," Suzan said anxiously, "I'll come later."

"I don't want you to come later!" He barked, "I am bloody locked in. I can't do it, I can't do it!"

"Throw the key through the cat flap, I'll try from outside." Suzan spoke carefully, aware of his trouble.

"Go and get the key in the shed!" he told her.

Suzan went to the shed to look for the key but could not find it.

Finally Ben unlocked the door. Thin and bloodless like a skeleton, yet a powerful anger in his eyes. Suzan helped him to lie down.

He told Suzan to call Max, his carpenter friend, to repair the lock.

"His number is written on the window sill," he said.

But she couldn't find the number.

"I can find a locksmith," Suzan suggested.

"I don't want to have a locksmith smelling of beer here!" he grumbled, which amused Suzan.

"Let's have some tea, shall we?" she said.

"Yes. That would be nice," he mumbled, his anger subsiding.

"Do you want me to straighten you up?" She bent over him.

"I don't want to straighten up." He shook his head from side to side. "I want to smoke. Can you go and get cigarettes for me? Buy a packet for yourself as well. You always smoke all my cigarettes. Also buy lunch and wine for yourself. Money is on the shelf." He behaved as if he wanted to pay for her care and not be indebted.

"I won't take money from the shelf," Suzan said flatly before she left for the shop.

29

The home care attendant rang Suzan up the next morning,

"Nothing to worry about," the tactful voice said, "Ben wants a word with you. Could you come here at quarter past ten?"

Suzan said she had an appointment at the bank at half past ten and that she would come at eleven.

At half past ten, Suzan went to see the bank manager, to discuss a loan. As she reached the counter, she suddenly felt sweaty and dizzy. She sprawled on a chair in the entrance hall before ringing the bell for the manager. 'It would be funny if I suddenly died,' she thought to herself. If she suddenly died, that is before him, it would be unfair. He would again have the heroic part, dying of cancer, looked after by several women, his ex-wife included, whereas her end would only be mundane, she would have a heart attack, waiting for a loan in a bank.

Luckily she was not having a heart attack. Only exhaustion and she tried to appear dignified while talking to the manager. The manager, a spry young man, self-important in a friendly way, asked her whether she would like her loan to be insured, so that if she was taken ill, and unable to work, the bank would pay her loan. Suzan did not want insurance.

As the manager filled in the form, she looked at her watch: ten to eleven. She told the manager she had an appointment at eleven. Could she come back later?

"You should have allowed yourself more time for this interview," the man said.

Suzan could not tell him that her dying ex-husband was expecting her at eleven. But she left the bank just the same and rushed to Ben's.

She was shocked to find a woman dressed in Bohemian clothes, sitting at his bedside, bent towards him, talking to him gently. Suzan greeted the woman coolly. Ben seemed surprised.

"Can you wait outside for a while?" he asked.

"No," Suzan said briskly. "I can't wait outside. It's raining. By the way, your home carer phoned me this morning and asked me to come here."

"Well…" He sighed.

"I can go, Ben," his guest said sweetly, "Can I come back in half an hour?"

"Okay," Ben grumbled.

When the woman went out, "She is a journalist," he told Suzan. "She was interviewing me." He pouted.

"Oh… Okay." Suzan regretted her reaction.

"The reason why I wanted you to come here this morning…" Ben expounded,. "Last evening I fell over," his husky voice trembled slightly, "It's the first time that's happened." He turned away his little face, "I am frightened, my love." Tears trickled from the inner edge of his eyes. It was for the first time that Suzan saw him admitting his fear. She held his hand. She kissed his forehead, his cheeks, as tears rushed down her cheeks.

"Do you want me to stay with you and cancel my trip?" she asked in a whisper.

"Yes," he said coyly, "Yes, stay here."

"Okay. I'll stay with you. I'll be very quiet. We will both be very quiet together. I'll go home now and come back in an hour."

The moment Suzan turned the door handle she was struck by a yellow rose being pushed through the cat flap. She delayed opening the door. Then she saw Tracy waiting in the yard. She came up to Suzan and put her arms around her, "It must be very difficult for you," she said.

"He is dying," Suzan moaned, then weeping, she yielded to Tracy's robust shoulder, and rested her face on it, seeking comfort and life.

30

The rain persisted all day and the wind howled. Suzan spent the whole afternoon sitting in Ben's antique armchair. While he slept, she often raised her face from the book she was reading – Henry Miller's *The Colossus of Maroussi* to look at him. She thought Ben would love this book, with its evocations of rural Greece and denunciations of modern civilization. And she lamented that the man who had never yielded to modern times would soon be gone.

He snored sometimes, his mouth open. Suzan thought he might die at any moment. How strange! She felt both sad and contented. Sad because she knew she would always miss him, and contented because they were at last truly together. And she felt she was no longer afraid of his death, no longer afraid of death at all.

At five o'clock, he woke up and seeing her sitting there with a book in her hand, wearing reading glasses, he smiled affectionately.

She gave him tea in the invalid cup she had bought for him. She helped him to sit up. He mocked her pronunciation:

"S't-up, s't-up! It sounds like 'Stop, stop.'"

She laughed. She put more cushions behind him and gave him the cup, demonstrating how to drink from it.

"Like a baby," she said.

He only took one sip, then shook his head. "I can't do it. It probably takes children six years to learn how to drink from it."

She poured tea into his Georgian cup, and with her help he drank from it.

"Shall we have some digestive biscuits?" he asked, a childish thrill in his weak voice.

She gave him a biscuit. He nibbled it slowly, carefully.

Watching him, Suzan felt he was returning to his origins, his beginning; a baby boy needing the care of a mother. And she felt like a mother. Her affection flowed towards a child, who was going to die. There would be no reward for her motherly sacrifice, no hope to see the child grow and benefit from her care.

"It was the best afternoon I've had since I've been ill," he suddenly announced cheerfully after eating his biscuit. Then he asked Suzan to come and sit on his bed. He wanted to tell her something. When she perched on the edge of his bed, he touched her hand and said, "Sorry, I can't leave you much money."

"I am not thinking of money," Suzan said dryly, getting up.

"Hang on. Listen to me."

She sat down again. He spoke in a matter of fact manner, "In my will I said you should get a third of the proceeds from my estate. And I have instructed Linda to give you 10,000 in cash immediately."

"Thank you," Suzan said calmly. She felt glad that he was leaving her some money and she was one of the beneficiaries of his estate. "I am not after the inheritance. But yes, I will expect fairness."

"It often happens that people are not happy with a will," Ben expounded.

He explained that the other two shares would go to Andy and Ben, Marsha's two sons. Suzan was taken aback. These two young men were connected with him only through Marsha, whom he had said, he never truly loved. Was Ben's motive a sense of guilt toward Marsha, who still carried the evidence of his destructiveness, whose face had been scarred in an accident on her way to Tamarisk some thirty years ago?

But Suzan refrained from questioning his decision. Now there was no time for questioning. He had chosen her as the sole companion for his dying moments and she was happy about their new relationship, perhaps closer than ever before.

She went to his place every morning at nine o'clock just after the nurse had washed him. She brought croissants from the bakery on her way and they had breakfast together. He now sat at the table with great difficulty and nibbled his croissant, holding it with his frail, trembling fingers.

She spent most of her days sitting on the white armchair, reading while he slept. She was expected to keep away intruders and provide the tranquillity he needed so much. She lit the fire at five in the afternoon, gave him a cup of tea and his pills, and prepared supper for him.

One morning she went to Ben's after 10 am. She found visitors there – Anthony and Iona, Ron's daughter. She was wearing a tiny deeply-cut white cotton top displaying her belly and back, her long silky hair flowing onto her tanned shoulders. Suzan was aware of Iona's visit, as Ron had told her in the street the other day, "Iona is coming down tomorrow, so she can cheer him up a bit." Yes, the girl sat there now, sparkling and relaxed, sure of her significance.

Then Richard, the frame-maker, came in. Suzan decided to go, do some shopping and come back later.

"Yes, come back at half eleven," Ben told her anxiously.

Coming back, Suzan found that Anthony, Richard and Iona were gone. The Macmillan nurse – the fat, blonde woman like some goddess of fecundity – was in the studio, talking to Ben.

"Shall I leave you alone?" Suzan asked the nurse.

"Yes, please," said the nurse with a gentle smile.

Suzan went to the garden and was surprised to see Iona there, sitting on the bench, weeping, her violin lying beside her. Suzan sat beside Iona, impelled to comfort her. She was now ready to forgive everybody, although a voice inside her protested, 'Why can't I hold onto my resentment?'

When the nurse left, Iona and Suzan went into the studio together. Iona went straight to Ben's bedside and sat down.

"I want to rest now," Ben said to her in a weak yet firm voice.

But Iona leaned over him and pressed her face to his, her lush silky hair covering his head, and whispered things in his ear. 'Just like Sharon,' Suzan thought. 'God knows what they are whispering. Are they asking him for something?'

Before leaving, Iona gave Suzan a gentle kiss on the cheek.

"I'll come again tomorrow," she said, as though expecting Suzan to be thankful.

After Iona left, Ben told Suzan that he had heard Iona playing a lament in the garden. He couldn't bear it, and sent the nurse into the garden to tell Iona to stop. "Lock the door and don't let anyone in. I'm tired of visitors," he finally said.

"I'll do my best," Suzan replied.

"Thank you."

She was overwhelmed by their finally-reached conspiracy. She made the fire and carried on with her reading, sitting in the white armchair.

Suddenly everything seemed good and harmonious: the pleasant heat of the iron stove, his sculptures and paintings dotted around, the silence, the now-clear sky, and Ben, so peacefully sunk into his dreams perhaps embellished by the morphine... How she wished that this quiet exaltation, this harmony would continue until his death, which was now galloping towards them.

When he woke up, she went to help him sit up. His bony body struggled under her caring hands, trying to prove its independence, its bravery. Holding his back and hand to help him straighten up, she sensed his embarrassment. His feet could not reach his slippers now, so she helped him to put them on.

"Are you practising yoga in bed?" a male voice burst in. It was Anthony who came in unexpectedly and without knocking.

113

"Yes," Ben gave a tired smile, then looking at Suzan, he cracked a joke, "You might even get aroused, my dear."

To this Anthony gave a robust chuckle.

Holding his hand, Suzan walked Ben to the table she had set for supper. Ben was eager to eat his pork pie, made by the wife of a painter friend.

"It's an art, making such a pie," he told Anthony. "I think the woman is more talented than her painter husband."

Anthony responded to that with a grin. Suzan cut the pie in tiny pieces so that Ben could eat it more easily. She placed the fork in his hand and helped him drink the glass of water with his pills. Now his hands had lost all their abilities and he was trying to hide his embarrassment.

After Anthony left, Suzan walked Ben to his armchair. She lit a cigarette and placed it between his lips, then she, too, had a cigarette. It was her first cigarette for years. They sat there opposite each other, quietly smoking.

"I'm not afraid of death any more," Ben spoke in a whispering voice, "I'm only afraid of being a bore. And I don't understand why people keep coming in, although I'm not able to entertain them any more."

"They like you," Suzan replied. "You shouldn't be embarrassed because you can't entertain people. We all enjoyed your company and your wit; now it's our turn to reciprocate. And people are coming because there is death for each of us and perhaps... perhaps they want to learn about death."

"Oh, that's why they are coming," Ben said, with an expression of astonishment and relief.

Suzan did not realise that by trying to justify people's visits, she jeopardised her own wish to be alone with him to the end.

Ben, animated and somehow reassured by her, told her that Richard's wife Donna had found a job as a secretary at a seal sanctuary. "So all the seals in their black suits and white cravats walked down the street behind Donna," he said, trying desperately to offer another proof of his entertaining talent.

31

When Sharon came the next morning and found Suzan already in the studio, she feigned a 'woman to woman' intimacy and showed Suzan her new spectacles with multicoloured rims. She told her how she had insisted on buying them, although the optician had tried to talk her out of them, saying that they were children's spectacles. As Sharon put the spectacles on to show her, giggling, the door creaked and opened slowly and who should walk in but Ursula. One of the German ex-girl friends... She had come last night from Worpswede to pay Ben a last visit and had stayed in a hotel in the High Street. Ben looked at Ursula with cold, reproachful eyes and told her that he wanted to go back to sleep. Ursula stood there by his bed, perplexed, then began to weep. Observing the scene, Suzan came and stood between them and bending towards Ben, she said gently, "I'll leave you alone with Ursula, so you can have a quiet talk."

"You don't need to go," Ben stated firmly, anguish in his eyes.

Ursula came close to Suzan and asked, "Did he say I should stay?"

"No," Suzan corrected her carefully, embarrassed at the accidental rivalry, "He told me I don't need to go."

Ben watched this confrontation between the two women with a glint of thrill in his weary eyes. Then Ursula walked to the door.

"He doesn't want to see me, he doesn't want to see me."

Hearing Ursula's trembling voice Suzan remembered the afternoon in Worpswede when she and Ben had a row and she had heard Ursula screaming downstairs in Ben's room, having an orgasm, unconcerned about Suzan's existence upstairs. But now Suzan was slowly becoming immune to all these reminders of betrayal. All she wanted now was a peaceful, grandiose finale.

She asked Sharon if she would take out the ashes from the stove so it could be lit in the late afternoon.

"I only clean the outside of the stove, I don't touch the inside," Sharon snapped, making it clear that she wouldn't take orders from the ex-wife of her dying master. She dusted some pictures instead, then walked to Ben, planted a quick kiss on his lips and left, bouncing like a little girl in her tight shorts, her frizzy hair tied in a ponytail.

Later that day, an envelope was pushed through the cat flap. Suzan went to fetch it without asking the deliverer in. She gave the envelope to Ben. But his fingers being stiff, he asked her to open it: a letter and a £100 note from Ursula. A farewell letter, an apology for her unannounced visit, ending with the words: 'Peace'.

"She owes me a lot of more than that," remarked Ben, looking at the £100 note. Ursula had bought two pictures from him in Worpswede and had not paid yet. "Put the money on that shelf," he told Suzan, "Hide it behind some books."

Suzan was surprised by this sudden cautiousness. Did he have evidence of Sharon stealing cash from him by now?

There was a knock on the door. It was an overweight fair young woman carrying a cardboard box. In the cardboard box was an emergency buzzer. She demonstrated and explained to Ben how to make it work. But a plug was needed. Suzan was more than willing to rush out and buy one. When she came back, the woman told her that Ben didn't want the buzzer after all. So she left. Ben stretched, lying in bed, held out his hand to the woman and politely thanked her.

In the evening, Suzan fried chicken breast and prepared tomato salad. She fed him as one would an infant. Ben surrendered to her care now and enjoyed the meal. She put him to bed and turned on Radio 3 for him: 'Romeo and Juliet' by Prokofiev. Listening to the music, a contented and serene expression settled on Ben's emaciated face. There he lay, immersed in the pleasures he had cherished all his life: music, art and love. And he seemed to want dissolve into them now, gently, with no regret.

That evening on her way home Suzan stopped at the Godolph Club. Lisa was there. She asked Suzan if she had warned Ben against Sharon.

"I'm absolutely sure that Sharon has already ripped him off!" Lisa said emphatically, eyes wide. "Look, I have a big home and six lodgers. I can't afford a proper holiday. I'm trying now to get the cheapest holiday for just a week. Sharon lives on income support, but she went on holiday five times within six months. She also bought a new van and her sons began to go to private piano lessons. Do you understand?"

"But Ben is not rich," said Suzan. "He has only got nine hundred pounds in his bank account, his statement came to my house recently."

"No, no," Lisa said, "Everyone knows that his last exhibition brought him a lot of money. Maybe he has more than one account and only the statements from his old account come to your house. How much money do you think Ben got from his last exhibition?" Lisa narrowed her sly eyes, while her tight lips expanded in an insinuating, malicious smile, "Of course she ripped him off."

"But what can I do now?" said Suzan.

"You must go to the police and get them to check Sharon's account. They will find a way to do it. The Government can check anyone's account at any time."

"I can't do that," Suzan looked away and a great tiredness came over her. How lonely she was, how powerless in the face of both worldly enemies, the opportunists, and the unworldly enemy: death.

"So she gets away with it and enjoys herself," Lisa went on, eager to agitate Suzan, "while, you, his companion and wife for so many years, live on a bank loan."

"Okay," Suzan ended up saying, "I'll talk to his executors about it."

The same evening, when Betty phoned her with her ever so sweet voice, Suzan told her of her suspicions about Sharon.

"Do you know how much money Ben has got on his account?" Suzan asked carefully.

"He has got sixty thousand pounds," Betty stated, caught off-guard. "I keep some of it with me and some is in his business account in the bank."

Suzan was startled.

"But he doesn't know that he has got that money," Suzan said.

"Well, tell him he has got money. All his paintings were sold."

Next evening, as they were sitting quietly near the stove after their dinner, smoking, Suzan told Ben what Betty had said about his money.

"Oh, no, she is mixed up!" he denied, "Anyway, why is she telling you this?"

"I'm just conveying the message. It's none of my business," Suzan spoke dryly.

He did not react and stared into the distance, mistrust and weariness in his eyes.

"I want to go to bed now," he finally mumbled.

She helped him to bed, covered him, put a light kiss on his lips.

"You don't need to come to do all these things, you know," he told her, "If you don't want to."

Damn! Suzan thought. He was becoming suspicious of her, while he resigned himself to other people's vicissitudes.

"I'll do everything I can, till the end," Suzan said, eager to regain his trust, his complete trust.

She decided not to be intoxicated by other people's materialism. And she wanted to show him that unconditional affection does exist. It would be her farewell gift to him. She wanted him to feel unconditionally loved by her and completely forgiven before he died. She wanted him to go to the other side of life without any guilt. With her unconditional love she wanted to counterbalance his increasing pain, his ultimate sentence. And she also wanted to rescue herself from guilt, for she might have contributed to his bitter end by putting the curse on him.

She tried hard now to disguise the intense emotions inside her, knowing that her emotions might lead him to a sense regret which he could not handle.

When she came in the morning, she greeted him like a nurse coming to do her job. Then she set out to perform, making a fire, making a cup of tea, helping him to get up and sit by the fire to have his tea.

"You make wonderful tea," he once whispered gently.

How she still loved his compliments, how she still needed his appreciation.

She was alert to all his movements, to all the signals; she now knew how to ease his strain, by getting up, by walking, by sitting up, by reaching out for his cap, for the ashtray, for his slippers, by using the knife and fork. How difficult all this was becoming for him! But as she knew his colossal pride, his passion for independence, she had to keep a careful balance, in order not to offend him. She behaved as coolly as possible when helping him, for he would be very annoyed if he detected any sense of patronizing authority in her gestures and expressions.

"Let me do it," she would say firmly and yet humbly.

He kept his proud, unyielding look while she was helping him in these details, cutting his burger into pieces, helping him to hold his glass, placing the white cotton napkin on his knee. He might well be indulging himself, she thought, in imagining himself a gentleman being helped by his servant. But she must not in any case hurt his dignity, the only value he could now cling to.

They ate mostly in silence. She knew he was concentrating on performing as well as he could the ritual of eating and she also knew he would suffer for his vanishing ability to tell jokes and stories if she attempted to entertain him. She did not want him to feel inferior, defeated. She did not want to challenge him, did not want him to think that she was now taking revenge by being strong and superior to him. But what a strain she was putting on herself! But she also enjoyed the sense of consent between them, as they ate in silence, without trying to have a good time, without trying to have fun, which had always been his existential obsession and an obstacle to true understanding.

Now they were just normal together, like a normal couple who had gone beyond seduction, beyond excitement, who had reached the comfort of routine, of practicality and companionship. Yet he still struggled at times to make her laugh.

"I am imagining a cartoon, a patient asking his doctor, 'Might I have a prescription for dying?'"

Or when he said, "It would make a good story; a rich man who is near to death spends all his money, distributes all his assets to other people, then is miraculously cured and realizes he has no money left to live on."

That evening after supper, Suzan cleared the table, gave him his morphine, and covered him with the duvet, just the way he liked. She told him to put his head, which was on the edge, in the middle of the pillow.

"I know what I'm doing," he grumbled.

"Sorry."

She switched on the radio for him.

"Oh, Sibelius!" he exclaimed, then gave all his attention to the music, ready to sink slowly into the depths of the sleep and of the unknown.

Suzan stroked his face and when her fingers touched his lifeless lips, his face darkened with disapproval, as though fearing the memories of love. He could no longer handle memories.

She turned off the light, crossing the dark room. By the door she turned round and called out sweetly: "Goodnight."

"Night-night," he called back childishly, gratefully.

As she climbed down the steps in the pitch dark, tears rushed to her eyes.

That afternoon, Suzan undressed him to put on his new pyjamas which Betty had bought for him. They had blue and pink stripes and were made of thin cotton.

"They are nice, aren't they?" he said, pointing to them, a wave of joy crossing his hollow face.

Although he struggled for a while to get into his new pyjamas, he soon gave up and yielded to her hands. She felt alienated from the skinny and white body, drained of flesh, of blood. It was an unfamiliar body, so different from the one she had known. As she directed his arms and legs into the pyjamas, she sensed his shame. Yet he escaped his shame by rendering himself a child again. His small, naked body was now in the hands of a mother. He was at her mercy. She tried to treat his skinny, weak body with great respect and not to hurt the pride he was so anxious to preserve. So she gently guided his wasted limbs into his new pyjamas. Then holding his hand, she led him to his chair. She made him sip his tea. After tea they remained seated in their usual corner. He sat upright and solemn, perhaps trying to retrieve his broken self-respect. Then his gaze wandered across the studio.

"Look, light!" he whispered with sudden enthusiasm, pointing to the pools of light in the middle of the room.

Perhaps in his imagination the mixture of shadow and light had transformed the room into a painting.

"I love your sculptures more and more," Suzan said, gazing around the room, wanting to enhance his sudden pleasure of life. "Especially my heads. There is a classical clarity about them." She got up and walked into the studio, "Look, this and this. Are they bronze?"

"No, alabaster," he corrected, "You can have them if you want."

"I did not say it with that intention," she mumbled, lowering her eyes. She feared he would corrupt her by offering her something material now, paying her for what she was doing. She didn't do all this in order to be paid. And why was she doing it? What motivated her alongside her love? Perhaps she was excited at a discovery. Perhaps she was discovering resources in herself, of which she was unaware.

"You can of course pay for them," she heard Ben expound prosaically.

Damn! He knew she had no money.

"I can't afford them," she murmured. "And I'm not interested in owning them."

He told her that Betty and Linda wanted to make some changes in his will, and that on Wednesday they would come with the solicitor to his place. Andy and Ben would also be present. He asked her if she would like to come to that meeting. Suzan said she'd rather not. He looked at her incredulously.

32

Nelly called in, Nelly tall, vigorous and dark-haired was from Northern Ireland and was once married to an artist who had let him down. Nelly never forgave her husband and never trusted artists. As they sat in the lounge having tea, she warned Suzan about her naïveté. She should think of her own interests, she told her. If not, there would be many people around who would take advantage of Ben now. This often happened, Nelly said, when those close to a dying person get too involved emotionally and lose their vigilance. "When you realise that you have been swindled by those people around him, it might be too late." Nelly's cool and realistic approach had an affect on Suzan. She began to think that she deserved that inheritance more than any other. She was the one who had given Ben the most. She had been exposed to his turbulent soul and was in many ways used by him. Used as the receptacle, used as a trigger, used as a muse... She had been involved with every part of his existence. And now she was fused with his perishing existence.

She told Nelly about the changes his two executors wanted to make to his will.

"I don't know what they will suggest. They might try to exclude me or diminish what I'm going to get."

Nelly, excited at playing the role of an adviser, dictated a codicil for Suzan, itemising paintings Ben had said he wanted her to have. She should contact a solicitor and her solicitor should contact Ben's solicitor, Nelly recommended.

As Nelly was leaving, Suzan pointed to the jugs on the shelf, "Take whatever you like, Nelly."

"Oh, I don't expect anything!" Nelly protested softly but still chose a crystal carafe.

In the morning, Suzan called a solicitor who agreed to pass on the contents of the codicil to Ben's solicitor.

When she went to his place in the morning she found a different nurse there, a white-haired, stocky woman with spectacles and a sweetly competent voice. She was getting ready to wash Ben, who was still in bed. Suzan went over to him.

"I'm very tired, my love," he whispered, his diminished shoulders bare, his face covered with a veil of infinite tiredness, of childish confusion.

"I shall come later," said Suzan, "After your wash."

"Come to tea," he called out softly as she walked to the door.

She returned half an hour later and found Ben dressed and sitting at the table over his croissants. The nurse was about to leave.

"I'm going on holiday," the nurse told him in a motherly coarseness.

"Have a nice holiday," he waved to her.

Suzan gave him the vitamins he was reluctant to take.

"But they're your three favourite colours," she said, "green, yellow, red."

"Okay," he said, "my favourite colours."

She insisted he should also have vitamin C powder.

"It will increase your strength," she said. "Tomorrow you will have a busy day."

He wanted to go to bed immediately. He struggled to rise from the table but could not. She stretched out her hand to him.

"Hold me by my waist," he said.

She put one of her arms around his delicate waist and held his hand. They walked slowly and cautiously to the bed. She helped him to lie down.

"Thank you," he murmured, "I'm already feeling better. I need clean handkerchiefs and a white shirt."

"Okay, I'll get them for you."

"Handkerchiefs are in the basement, in the first right-hand drawer."

A pile of dirty clothes lay on the floor in the basement, left there by Sharon, who had not taken them to her house for washing. Sharon had apparently lost interest in him after taking as much as she could. So why care about a dying man any longer?

Suzan took the clothes to the launderette and did shopping for him. She bought porridge, sheep's yoghurt and peaches, she thought would be good for his digestive system.

Returning to the studio, she prepared the porridge and peeled a peach, cut it into small slices. She set the table for him, not forgetting a clean napkin in a silver ring.

When he took the first spoonful of his porridge, he said it should be cooled by milk.

"Okay, I'll go and get milk."

"Do you mind?"

"Not at all."

She rushed out to the supermarket. She wouldn't tell him where she had bought the milk from, because she knew how he hated supermarkets.

In the queue she became nervous, thinking of him waiting at the table, in front of his plate of porridge.

"Do you mind if I go ahead of you?" she asked the woman in front, who had a full trolley. She showed to the woman the pint of milk she was holding.

"My husband is ill. I'm buying it for him. He's on his death bed, actually"

"Oh, I'm sorry," the woman whispered, stepping back.

Suzan was out of breath when she opened the door of the studio. But to her disappointment she found him spooning up the last bit of porridge.

"It was very good, I enjoyed it without milk," he said.

She had no choice but to smile. She put the milk in the fridge and walked him to bed.

Early that afternoon Betty came. She opened the door quietly, saw Ben sleeping and signalled to Suzan to come out. Suzan joined her in the yard. There was resentment in Betty's eyes. Perhaps because Suzan had taken away the role Betty was so keen to play. The role of an angel.

Betty asked her to pass on a message to Ben. Suzy, the journalist who had interviewed him a few days ago, should come to their meeting concerning his will tomorrow. Suzan could not penetrate the mystery behind Betty's suggestion. Betty had always tried to put other women in Ben's perspective, thinking perhaps that if she herself could not take Suzan's place, another woman might. But this could not be Betty's motive right now, since he was a dying man, Suzan concluded. But then what was Betty's intention by wanting to include that woman journalist into his will?

Yet Suzan promised Betty to pass on her message to Ben. Thanking her, Betty left. Suzan observed her from behind. And it occurred to her stronger than ever before that there was a sad incongruity about Betty: her thin, twisted legs in black leggings in sharp contrast to her disproportionately large, masculine shoulders. And the contrast was in Betty's character, too.

At seven Ben suddenly opened his eyes and asked animatedly, "Are we going to have a sandwich?"

"Yes! We shall! We shall!" Suzan replied in a sing song voice.

As she was setting the table, Linda arrived, smiling broadly as usual.

Ben received her with a grumpy stare. She was unexpected. But Suzan, embarrassed by his rudeness, asked Linda if she would like to have tea and a sandwich.

"Tea would be nice. But no sandwich, thank you," Linda said, "I'm going to treat myself to an Indian takeaway before going to Betty's."

"Call Betty, tell her you have arrived and ask her if she wants an Indian, too," Ben grumbled glaring at her.

Linda phoned Betty who said yes, she would like an Indian meal, because the stew she was preparing had burnt. Then Linda sat back at the table, determined to make herself at home, and started a long speech, telling them that the weather was nice in Lewes, that the rain had started half way through her journey, that she had had two breaks before she arrived in Heathertown, had had Cornish cream tea in a café in St Austell etc.

Ben fixed an intensely contemptuous stare on Linda as she talked nervously, giggling at times. But Linda, seemingly determined not to be intimidated by him any longer, talked on and on. Finally she said she had brought Italian pasta with her and was going to cook for him tomorrow.

"Suzan is looking after me," Ben turned his face to Suzan and a wistful smile crossed his face.

"But I can cook pasta nonetheless," Linda expounded, "If you don't eat it we will." She grinned, looking at Suzan, expecting her support. She seemed more defiant towards Ben than ever before. The great man she had hopelessly admired and loved, was now a skinny man in pyjamas and his once resonant voice was weakened by disease.

Ben began to eat the sandwich Suzan had cut into small pieces for him. However, when Linda said that she would arrange all his paperwork for him tomorrow, his hostile expression subsided.

"That would be nice," he said. "Come tomorrow, after half past nine."

After Linda had left, Suzan led Ben to their usual after-dinner corner by the window to have a cup of tea and a cigarette.

"Did you notice how rude, how mean Linda is?" Ben finally blurted out. "She is offered free accommodation by Betty, and instead of asking Betty what she could bring for dinner, she decides to have an Indian. For God's sake! She has always been like that, this woman! I hate her!"

Suzan refrained from commenting, knowing the arbitrariness of his judgements and emotions. With this in mind, she touched upon the subject that had been on her mind all day.

"I wouldn't mention this if you hadn't told me about your will," Suzan said. "But then yesterday I wrote down the details concerning your will."

"Why?" He shot her a forbidding glance.

"Just in case—"

"Are you going to blackmail me now?" He shouted interrupting her, which threw her off balance.

"Why should I blackmail you? I only wrote them down because you articulated them. And because I noticed you are becoming a little forgetful under the influence of the morphine…"

"Are you questioning my mental state?" he yelled, his hollow face turning wild. Once again he placed himself on a battlefield and targeted her from his trenches.

"I knew such unpleasantness was due to come, that all the people I have tried to be fair to would start fighting each other."

"It's not the case," Suzan tried to calm him. "Everybody is in agreement with your arrangements. All I did was write down your offerings. I'd rather you took my name completely out of your will. I don't care. Believe me, what I am doing for you has nothing to do with that. I was ready to go to Paris without asking you for anything. And I was always afraid you would misinterpret my care. I am only doing it because…" She rose and walked towards the kitchen. "Please don't give me anything. Anything!" Her voice went high. Then, after a moment of silence she added quietly, turning to him. "But I'll still do what I can until the end."

"I know that." He was calm now. "But I don't like being told what to do."

"I am not telling you to do anything. I was just documenting your wishes in case others denied them. They are not my friends, you know. They are only your friends."

There was silence again. He continued to smoke, staring into the distance. Then he slightly bent over and in his confusion pressed his cigarette into the cream bowl, rather than into the ashtray.

Seeing him do this, Suzan thought cruelly to herself: 'there is no harsher punishment than cancer itself.'

Suddenly tears burst out of her eyes. She cried because she failed to be completely reconciled to him, to be reconciled to herself. Because she did not want to think her years with him as a waste. She wanted to tell him that no money in the world could pay off her years with him, her love, her pain...

Looking at the cream bowl in disgust, Ben said that he was very tired.

Suzan helped him to bed. She covered him carefully and stroked his forehead.

"Everything will be all right," she whispered, bending over him. "Everybody respects you. You have done a good job. You will be recognised and appreciated. And I am sorry if I have upset you."

"Thank you," he murmured gently, preparing for a long night's sleep.

"Shall I put the urine bottle near your bed, so that you don't have to get up, just in case?" she asked.

"Okay, that's a good idea." He yielded for the first time to the urine bottle, the most humiliating evidence of his decay.

Suzan placed the plastic bottle on the bedside table.

She bent over to kiss him goodbye.

"You must have eaten onion again." He turned his face slightly away.

"No I didn't," she said, "Your nose is oversensitive."

"Everybody smells of onion these days," he said.

Suzan knew he was tired of people, of everybody, because he was tired of himself, of his own dying body.

33

Marsha insisted on visiting Ben, although Ben had instructed Betty to discourage all the visitors. He told her that he didn't want to see anybody any more. But only the next day, about midday, Marsha walked in, rather defiantly. She was wearing a man's shirt and baggy trousers, her curly grey hair was stylishly cut.

Suzan showed her to the seat by Ben's bed. Although Ben was in a deep sleep, Marsha kissed him on the lips and held his hand tightly so that he should wake up and see her. Suzan had no choice but remain in the background, sitting in the armchair, trying to read, trying not to make Marsha feel observed. But Marsha wouldn't have taken any notice of her anyway.

Ben opened his eyes after ten minutes or so and smiled. "I didn't know you were here," he murmured.

Marsha gave him another kiss on the lips, held his hand in hers. "I know you don't want visitors. But I'll only stay twenty minutes," she told him in saccharine voice.

Suzan got up and said, "I shall leave you to have a quiet talk together."

She went out and returned an hour later, assuming Marsha had already gone. But to her surprise, she found them engaged in whispered conversation, Marsha beaming. Suzan had the intuition that Ben was making her some offer, perhaps telling her what he was going to leave to her.

Suzan seated herself in the armchair, expecting Marsha to leave. Ben looked over to Suzan and said in a clear loud voice, "I want to talk to Suzan."

He repeated this three times. At this, Marsha got up and went out to wait in the yard.

Suzan was pleased and she sat by him.

"I want to talk to Suzan," Ben persevered.

"Yes, you want to talk to me," Suzan said.

"Not you to me, but I to you," he said.

"Okay, you talk to me, I am listening," Suzan said.

"Don't listen. I am talking to you," he said.

"Yes," Suzan said, patiently.

"I want to talk to Suzan. To Suzan. I mean to Marsha," he went on, his eyes glassy and wide open. Suzan knew that he was lost.

"Oh. Okay. I'll go and fetch her," Suzan said, slightly hurt. She went down to the yard and found Marsha walking up and down, her arms folded, an expression of exhilaration on her face.

"He wants to talk to you," Suzan told her.

"Oh!" Marsha beamed and rushed upstairs.

Suzan sat on the bench to wait. Half an hour passed. She began resenting the fact that Marsha, like the others, took advantage of her tolerance and capitalized on it. Her sensitivity was probably interpreted by them as capitulation. Realizing this, Suzan decided to change this unfair deal and went upstairs. As she opened the door, a word spoken by Ben in a whisper struck her: "Money."

Marsha, holding his hand, was nodding, a slow smile stretching across her wrinkled face. She was obviously now anxious to be recompensed for the hurt, the pain and the stress he had caused her in the past.

Suzan walked to the armchair. Ben, turning his face, cast a sharp, mad glance at her and said, "Leave us alone."

My God! This was the reward! This was the reward for her trying to provide him with all possible comfort and peace of mind.

"Why don't you attend him for a few hours, so I can go home and take a rest?" Suzan said to Marsha in a hostile tone of voice.

"I can't," Marsha spoke rather disdainfully. "I've got to get back home."

"Okay. I'm going to wait in the garden then," Suzan said coldly and left.

As she was sitting in the garden, Marsha came out and laid a hand on her arm.

"He is confused," she said, "It must be very hard for you. He sent me to calm you down. He thinks you are upset."

Suzan forced a smile.

"I'm not upset."

"I'm glad," said Marsha, "Do come up."

"Thank you," Suzan replied. But seeing Marsha go back to the studio, she scolded herself, 'Why do I yield so easily?' She stayed in the garden for another twenty minutes, then returned to the studio.

They were still talking in whispering voices. But Ben, noticing Suzan, broke off and said to her in a juvenile tone, "I was telling Marsha about you and me. There is nothing to talk to Marsha about, but you and me, Suzan and Ben. You and me. No one else. Suzan and Ben."

This was the most unambiguous declaration of love Suzan had ever heard from him. She came closer, laid her hand gently on his humid forehead, and whispered: "Fine. Everything's fine."

But Marsha, obviously hurt about this declaration, took Ben's hand lying on his chest, and held it in both her hands.

But Ben fixed his veiled stare stubbornly on Suzan, as though afraid of losing his focus, of being derailed, and repeated in a clear, assertive tone: "There is nothing between Marsha and me. I was only talking about you and me, Suzan and Ben."

"That's rather sad, Ben." Marsha forced a smile.

Ben did not respond to this. Marsha took her leave.

Linda phoned shortly before midnight. She told Suzan that Alan, Ben's dealer, was angry with Gisela and Reinhard who had taken some pictures with them as they left for

Germany. But Linda said that Alan was wrong because Gisela and Reinhard had helped Ben a lot in the past and that he liked them.

Suzan contradicted Linda, saying that Ben had already generously reciprocated their help and had given them several pictures while in Worpswede. Suzan had seen those pictures hanging on the wall of their house.

Linda did not react to this.

Suzan asked Linda casually whether she had seen the £100 on the shelf because she had looked for it this morning and could not find it where Ben had told her to leave it.

"Oh," Linda sounded startled. "Yes. I took the £100 and all the money from the blue bowl because I have to buy things for Ben."

Suzan was speechless.

Soon after she put down the receiver, the phone rang again. Now Betty was on the line, asking Suzan to give her own phone number to the night nurse, so the nurse could call her when Ben died.

"Are you willing to be with Ben at the moment of dying?" Betty asked in a rather matter-of-fact tone of voice.

"Of course," Suzan replied.

"Oh, good." Betty gave a sigh of relief. Suzan could not help but think how, till recently, Betty had insisted on visiting him every evening at seven, preventing Suzan from sharing the best time of the day with him, the time when the morphine made him animated and talkative. Betty had enjoyed the last resources of his company, but now expected Suzan to rush to him whenever called by the night nurse. Now all the women who had come to see him on his death bed had returned to their normal lives and obligations, or had gone on holidays, but Suzan would remain with him till his last breath and this made her feel oddly triumphant.

As she was unable to go to sleep after these two calls, she decided to return to Ben's.

It was a quiet and warm night with a full moon. On the radio it had been announced that flooding was expected if the wind came up and the high pressure dropped. The high street, bordered by old Georgian and Edwardian cottages, was shining dimly in the moonlight. There was no one in sight. Not a soul. Only Suzan walking in the street, in her long skirt, the grating sound of her flat leather shoes echoing on the deserted cobblestones. The town looked cosy and charming so late at night. Looking up at the full moon, which wandered amongst patches of cloud, Suzan could not help but remember their passionate full moon nights at Tamarisk. In the bedroom up the ladder, lit by the moon, their bodies, so hot and shamelessly alive... And now staring at the full moon, she felt as if supported by the moon and she felt proud that she had no other motive than love that made her walk in the deserted streets so late at night.

A middle-aged nurse in a blue uniform was sitting on the armchair reading a book.

Ben was awake. Seeing Suzan, he appeared amazed.

"What time is it?" he asked hastily, whispering.

"Quarter past two." Suzan smiled.

"Oh, I thought nine." He widened his eyes, "What happened?"

"I couldn't sleep," Suzan laid her hand over his closed hands.

"Why?"

"Because I was thinking of you, I'll spend the night here." Suzan spoke softly.

"Will she stay too?" Ben pointed childishly to the night nurse.

"Yes."

"What's going on? I don't understand?" He gazed around.

The nurse got up and joined Suzan by the bedside.

"*Alles in Ordnung*," Ben said to the nurse.

"I beg your pardon?" the woman asked gently.

"He speaks German," Suzan explained.

"Oh!" the nurse smiled shyly and returned to her chair.

"Does she know English?" Ben asked, meaning the nurse.

"Yes," Suzan said, "She is English."

"Does she understand?"

"Yes, she does."

Then his gaze went over to the nurse as he addressed her: "Do you mind if Suzan speaks English?"

"No," said the nurse gently.

"She might also stay here," Ben said to Suzan, meaning the nurse. "She knows. She is a doctor."

"Yes," Suzan said. "Yes, my love," and laid a comforting hand on his forehead. "Do you want some water?"

"Yes, give me water." He spoke rather robustly.

As she gently lifted his now smaller, lighter head, the nurse joined her and put a napkin on his chest, "Do you want me to do it?" she asked.

"I can do it," Suzan said, not wanting to involve the nurse in their little affectionate ritual as she watched him drinking avidly from the tiny crystal glass, his eyes sparkling with desire for the water. Afterwards she gently placed his head onto the pillow. Then, seeing how dry his lips had become, she smeared Vaseline on them.

"Very good," he said in a formal tone, "That's very good. Thank you."

How rewarding!

"I feel very hot. I want to cool off." He puffed.

Suzan took off the duvet and lightly stroked his feet. He had a fever. She wetted a napkin with water and placed it on his forehead.

"That's very good." He spoke earnestly.

She felt proud that she was doing the right things for him and that he appreciated it. The nurse, feeling perhaps a little redundant, came to take over the job.

"He's all right," Suzan said. No one, no one else understood his needs better than she, Suzan thought proudly.

She knew all about him: his body, his mind, his soul. She knew him better than anyone else in the world. And now she could provide him with comfort in the way no one else could. Because all she did was directed by affection and intimacy. But she also wanted him to admire her skills. She wanted to make herself unique for him, at last, at last. And she did not want to allow the night nurse to prove herself more efficient than she.

"I want to get up," Ben announced out of the blue.

She wished she had the strength to lift him and carry him. But she remembered what the other Macmillan nurse had said the day before: "He is not to get up any more."

"Sorry, Ben. You can't get up," Suzan said. What a punishment for a man who was always in command, who could always come and go when and wherever he wanted.

"Ales girls," Ben said to himself, then glancing up at Suzan, he added, "It is a nice word isn't it? It's a biblical term. Do you read the bible?"

"No," Suzan said, "You know that I have no religion but I believe in God. Do you believe in God?"

He turned his face away and mumbled stubbornly: "No."

Suzan felt regret that he had no faith whatsoever. How lonely he must be feeling now, on his journey to the unknown. But she also felt a kind of admiration for him because he maintained his position to the end and refused to compromise.

Suzan went to relax at the back of the studio, which was reserved for making sculptures. She sat on the wooden floor which smelt of plaster. She raised her hand, waving to him playfully, "I'm here!"

He acknowledged her with anxious eyes.

"Do you mind if I eat my sandwiches?" The nurse's little voice was raised.

Suzan looked across and saw the nurse with a sandwich and a tiny box of fruit juice in her hand.

"No, of course not," Suzan replied, "I don't mind anything at the moment."

She suddenly felt calm and safe, seeing the nurse having her sandwich and fruit juice. At last she shared her grief with a woman, who had no reason for rivalry. They were alien to each other and yet unified around a dying man, in late night quietness, while outside a full moon wandered in the dark sky.

Suzan heard Ben's moaning, "I can't sleep."

She went to him and sat on the edge of his bed.

"That's okay. Just relax, my love. It's a beautiful night. It's a full moon."

Memories rushed back again, memories of full-moon nights, of shared euphoria, of shared joy of life. They both believed in the energy and desire of full-moon nights.

He looked at her in awe, trying to understand what she meant when she mentioned the full moon. But suddenly the look in his glassy eyes turned hostile.

"I am not a liar," he said.

Suzan was taken aback. Then she bent over him and laid her cheek gently against his and whispered: "No. You are not a liar."

And suddenly she believed it. Suddenly she admitted that he had not lied to her when he flirted with other women. On the contrary he had tried hard to be sincere. He believed that fidelity was not in his nature, even that fidelity was not natural. But when he told her that he liked flirting with women, but never made love to another woman while he was married to her, she did not believe him and that's when she said, "Liar." Now she felt ashamed for having said that. Now she believed him and loved him unreservedly, as she sat at his bedside, at three o'clock in the morning, in the dimly-lit hallow studio, with a full moon outside.

"No, you are not a liar, my love," she repeated. He was not a liar, she again admitted. He invented and created his own truth. And he defended what he had invented and created. And now all his sins were washed away.

"But you said I am a liar," he persevered in a quarrelsome tone.

She suddenly realised that deep inside him was still a yearning to experience true feelings, feelings he had lost perhaps long ago. Maybe the time when he was a little child, trying to understand what a war meant, as he was alone in that cold attic as an evacuee. It was perhaps then that he had lost belief in the human race.

"I was wrong," Suzan said.

"What's going on? I don't understand," he gazed around. Then his eyes, sharp, deep, alert, yet forlorn eyes, fixed on her and he said, "You are not telling the truth."

His words suddenly hurt Suzan. How typical of him, this kind of projection, this kind of manipulation. Why her affection could not reach him, could not finally transform him?

She decided to go home and get some sleep. She told the nurse to phone her anytime if Ben needed her. Then she placed a light kiss on Ben's forehead, rested her cheek on it for a moment, and said softly, "See you later."

"Where are you going?" he asked in an alarmed tone of voice, fear glowing in his wide open eyes.

"Home," she said.

"Home?" he echoed in a whisper, awe in his expression. He appeared to be wondering what 'home' meant. He was homeless now. He belonged nowhere, suspended between pain of life and fear of death.

As she left, she shuddered with guilt. She should not leave him. She stood on the wooden step for a while and listened to silence. The smell of distant sea and wet grass reached her. She lifted her face to the sky. The full moon reigned more glamorously than ever in the clear crisp sky.

34

When Suzan returned to Ben's at nine thirty in the morning, she found Betty sitting at his bedside.

"He is very agitated," Betty said. And leaving the chair to Suzan, she walked to the dining table and busied herself with some paperwork.

Ben's eyes were watery, remote and grim. His folded legs were moving spasmodically under the duvet. Suzan carefully unfolded them. He was pulling the duvet to his midsection, where his bowels were. His tiny chest was exposed, the top of his pyjamas slid to one side. Suzan held his hand. He grasped it with a strength she had not anticipated and looked at her in recognition.

"Dear Ben, my dear Ben," she whispered. "Soon it will be over, soon it will be peace and quiet."

She laid her hand on his forehead. A moment of relaxation, a moment of surrender, of hope.

She noticed the morphine box was empty.

"Can you call the Macmillan nurses and tell them to come and renew the syringe?" she said to Betty.

"Oh, that's what it is," said Betty and phoned the nurse.

Suzan, sitting on Ben's bed, leaned her legs against his wriggling, thin body and tried to comfort him further.

"All this will be over soon, my darling. There will be no more pain."

Some sounds formed in his throat and muffled words came out, "Why is it happening?"

She could not answer. But watching him, his tiny body diminished, moving his hand desolately from his bowel region to his mouth, then to his bowel again, clasping the duvet, while his face gave signals of unbearable pain, she shuddered, thinking how he had been obsessed by female bodies and ignored the soul within. She, too, had been an image he himself had created, according to his needs. He had formed an arbitrary image of her, and then forced that image upon her. In a way, he had deprived her from herself. Now, watching him, Suzan felt she had lost her independence again, now absorbed by his death. The more his body diminished, the closer she felt to him. And her affection for him became greedy, insatiable. She wanted to pour into him all her affection to relieve him from his pain. And it worked, even though his body still gave off signals of pain, his face grew serene every time she stroked his forehead and held his hand. Their eyes met. Again words gurgled in his throat, trying to reach his tongue, "Suzan. Don't go."

He was startled by Betty's voice: "I must go and mail some cheques," Betty was saying.

Suzan nodded distractedly. She wanted Betty to go away; she wanted everybody to go away. She wanted to be alone with him, alone in their underworld. She detected a sign of relief in his expression when the door closed; he knew Betty had gone and the two of them were alone now.

Again, he wrestled with words and clasping her hand, said, "Don't go."

"I'm not going anywhere," she whispered. "I will be here with you. I'll be with you always."

He turned his face away. Behind his dry, closed eyelids were tears. Tears of love and regret? Tears of gratitude and anger? Anger that it was no longer possible to be together?

Looking at his lean, noble profile, Suzan found herself reviewing his faults and virtues: his arrogance, deceptiveness, cruelty, egotism; then, his virtues marched forth, his legendary virtues: his charm, his enthusiasm, his generosity, his gallantry, his boundless creativity.

Before her was now a half-dead tiny body, a drained face. And she felt she had never loved any other human being as much as she loved the man dying before her, a man devoid of flesh… And she now felt ready to send him away, before anything could spoil this immaculate intimacy.

She placed the tip of a cotton swab into his dry mouth and dripped water. His lips closed and he sucked the wet cotton. She repeated this several times. Then words rolled out of his throat: "That's nice."

Two nurses arrived. One male, one female. They renewed the syringe, and while they were doing this, Ben's cloudy eyes searched for Suzan. Suzan leaned towards him so he could see she was there. She smiled at him and rested her hand on his sweaty forehead.

The male nurse said flatly: "He won't wake up again today."

Suzan sat again on his bed and leaned her leg against his trembling side, caressed his skinny arm, stroked his humid hand. She whispered, "We will be together to the end."

The highest affection is that which is offered to a dying person, that's the moment a human being craves affection most. Looking at him, at his perishing body, Suzan felt not only affection, but also respect. She respected his life, full of struggles, failures, victories, illusions, pleasures, excitement, art, passion – all this was woven into the tapestry of his life. A tapestry which was now being torn apart, knot by knot, thinning, loosening. But Suzan believed either a bird or a deer was to be born from the remaining essence, and that she was trying to contribute to this birth.

Betty took turns with Suzan so that Suzan could go home and rest for a few hours. When she returned in the afternoon, Betty told her that they had put him on a morphine machine. In her kind and impersonal tone of voice, Betty explained that now he would be given a regular dose of morphine through the machine while asleep, and would thus be free of pain to the end. Then she left with an air of accomplishment.

Suzan spent a few hours in the studio, sitting in her armchair, waiting for Ben to wake, so she could give him his tea and porridge.

When the doctor came – a tall man with a round gentle face and pale, remote eyes – Suzan asked him whether she needed to give Ben any medication when he woke up.

"He won't wake up any more," the doctor said.

Suzan, stupefied, asked in a whispering tone: "Never?"

"He will go peacefully in his sleep," replied the doctor and laid his hand briefly on her shoulder, "There is nothing we can do any more." A chilling yet tender smile on his face, he went out and drove off.

'He hated machines all his life and now he has surrendered to a machine,' Suzan found herself thinking, staring at the tiny, square machine, leaning on his side, linked through a needle pinned to his chest.

She went to the garden, walked up and down the orchard; tiny apple trees already loaded with red and green apples. What a beautiful view! The orchard, the last image he had created: an orchard among the dilapidated stone buildings, and in the distance the green, hilly landscape divided into geometrical squares. How impossible it would be not to miss him. How impossible to ignore the many images he had spread around him. Now he was sleeping, linked to a tiny, black morphine machine, overtaken by an anarchic army of cancer cells creeping into every corner of his defeated body.

When Suzan returned to the studio that evening, after spending some hours wandering like a sleepwalker in Portlando valley, she found the friendly, plump nurse sitting on the armchair, knitting.

"I am very upset," Suzan told the nurse, "They should have told me he wouldn't wake up any more. I was here yesterday all day and all night. Why didn't they tell me they were going to put him on the morphine machine? I could have said goodbye to him."

She suddenly burst into tears. The nurse came to her.

"I am sorry, my love," she said, in a broad Cornish accent, "They should have told you. But he can still hear you. Sit there. Talk to him. I'll leave you alone, I'll go and smoke a cigarette outside." And she left, dragging her heavy buttocks and thick legs towards the door.

Suzan sat on the chair beside the bed, and put her hand on Ben's lifeless hand.

"Ben, dear Ben, I love you," she whispered, tears streaming down her cheeks, her nose running. She had never said to him that she loved him when he was strong, passionate and healthy, because she had realised that the moment he was sure of her love, he would look down on her, turn away from her. She regretted that they had never truly believed in each other's love. Because in truth he did not believe in love, maybe because he was so preoccupied by images, by performance. He was both the hero and the director of the play.

But now he had deserted the stage. Now she was alone on the stage and could tell him that she loved him Now, she could tell him the truth. Now, when it was not possible for him to respond...

"I love you," she continued, still crying. "I love you. Forgive me that I have never told you this before."

As she bent over him, still talking to him and crying, something miraculous happened. His eyelids parted slowly and his head moved towards her. His faded eyes searched for her. Then, for a split second, they looked into each other's eyes. It was their closest meeting ever. But then Suzan caught a gleam of reproach in his dim, forlorn eyes, perhaps because she was now alone on the stage, without him.

Suddenly she felt nervous that her nose was running and that her face might appear ugly to him, the face that had been the model of so many portraits.

She tried to smile at him, for she wanted him to take her smiling face with him. She wanted to secure his admiration in the afterlife.

"Have a safe journey," she whispered, caressing his hair, his cheeks, his hands.

He closed his eyes slowly and turned his face away in a meaningful way, in a stylish way, aware of the finale. Then he sank into a deep, mysterious sleep.

The nurse entered.

"Thank you," Suzan said as she rose. "He did hear me. He opened his eyes."

"Really?" the nurse's round white face froze in amazement.

That night at ten o'clock Betty phoned.

"How are you?"

"I'm all right," Suzan replied coldly.

"I spoke to the Macmillan nurse," Betty went on, "The nurse said that he can still hear in his sleep. So you can go and talk to him."

"I already did," Suzan said, sensing Betty's sense of guilt.

"I am so glad," Betty sighed, "You were so close to him. And you have been so good to him. You deserve a medal."

There was a silence, a silence loaded with unspoken vindictiveness, unspoken forgiveness.

Then, changing the subject, Betty told Suzan about a list dictated by Ben some time ago to determine the distribution of his possessions, and about his wish that a party should be given at his place after the funeral and that ham sandwiches, sherry and Irish whiskey should be offered.

"So he organized everything," said Suzan.

"Yes," Betty gave a gentle laugh.

Suzan asked whether he had given any instructions about who should be the chief mourner.

"No," answered Betty.

"I'll be the chief mourner then," said Suzan firmly.

"Of course," Betty replied.

Then Suzan asked why Linda had not turned up although she had promised to come on Friday.

"She phoned this morning. She'll come on Sunday," said Betty with a hint of exasperation. "Oh, she is so selfish this woman, so inconsiderate, so bossy. Now she wants to be the centre of everything. Oh, I can't stand it! I will make it clear to her this time."

Suzan was amazed at Betty's massive verdict and her burst of anger. Perhaps because her kindness was so contrived, her anger was so massive, so ruthless, Suzan thought.

"It's difficult for me to judge," Suzan said, avoiding the conspiracy.

To this, Betty reacted diplomatically.

"I think we all should be united now. We should work together to do everything the way Ben would have wished."

"Yes," Suzan replied flatly.

"I am so glad, Suzan, that you have kept in contact with me," Betty finally said gently.

35

Three Macmillan nurses in blue uniforms walked in; two of them young, obviously trainees. The older nurse said they had come to clean him and change the needle of the morphine machine. Suzan left Ben's bedside, and went over to where Betty and Marsha stood in chit chat.

The older nurse guided the young ones in changing the napkin. As Suzan cast a glance toward the bed, she caught the glimpse of the napkin and of Ben's tiny bottom being wiped by delicate hands. She was so embarrassed by the way he was handled now. He, who had so admired women's bodies, was now prepared for death by the hands of two young women who were perhaps trying to capture some sense of spiritual elevation out of their menial task. Their murmurs rose above the heavy, melancholy silence surrounding the dying body.

Then something miraculous happened. A powerful shout burst out and shook the air. Ben, medically unconscious, suddenly yelled at the nurses,

"Don't touch me! Don't touch me! For Christ's sake! Leave me alone! Go away! All of you!"

The nurses obviously shocked, withdrew and stood there, confused and helpless. Then the older nurse came close to him again, bent over him and spoke sweetly, "It won't take long, love. We have to change the needle."

Ben placed his hand firmly on the spot where the needle had been, his eyes still closed. His lips curled in a sneer, he remained unyielding. Then the nurse came over to Suzan, knowing she was the one closest to the dying man.

"He won't let us change the morphine needle," she said gently, "Could you help us?"

Suzan walked to the bed. Ben still held his hand stubbornly on the left side of his chest, refusing the needle. She turned to the nurses and said:

"You are bothering him. There are too many of you. Just one is enough."

At this, the older nurse stood next to Suzan, with a needle in her hand while the other two kept their distance.

Suzan put her hand on Ben's forehead, knowing the soothing effect, and whispered, "My love, let me do it, will you?"

Then she touched his hand and his hand yielded to her. It was his act of total surrender to her, the most genuine recognition. Suzan carefully lifted his obedient hand and placed it in the middle of his chest. Then she bent over and placed her lips gently on his sweaty forehead.

The nurse watched the scene, wonderstruck. Then, while Suzan enclosed his hand in hers, keeping her other hand on his forehead, the nurse plunged the needle into the thin skin.

36

Early the next morning Suzan was awakened by Betty's call. Betty had been at Ben's since seven o'clock.

"I think he would be pleased to hear your voice," Betty said in a sweet voice, "He is talking to you all the time."

"I am coming immediately."

Suzan rushed to the studio.

Betty readily gave her seat to Suzan, and they exchanged a look of sad acknowledgment, of kinship.

Ben was still unconscious and in pain. As soon as Suzan took his hand, he clasped hers and immediately her name came rolling out of his mouth. Then other words, muffled and indistinguishable.

She bent over him, watching him breathing, each breath carrying a faint whistling sound. She felt as if she was helplessly watching a sinking ship full of treasure. A treasure of precious words, precious images, precious sensations, precious wit…

He brought his hand to his mouth, which was sore and dry. She put a wet swab in his mouth and he eagerly sucked the cotton tip, like a baby sucking milk. She dropped some anti-infection drops onto his tongue, and softly rubbed his lips with Vaseline. He kept his mouth open and she continued to give him water with a swab.

The signs of pain increased. Suzan told Betty to call the doctor. As Betty was trying to reach the doctor on the phone, Marsha walked in and hurried over to Ben's bed and laid a hand on his forehead.

Ben frowned.

"Let me sit by him," Marsha said to Suzan.

"No. Can't you see? He is clasping my hand."

"He can clasp my hand," Marsha said imposingly.

"I shall wait till he relaxes," persevered Suzan. Ben's grasp on her hand tightened. Suzan could see the frown of disapproval behind his tightly closed eyes. It occurred to Suzan that he would be irritated now by Marsha's touch, a touch tainted with vengeance and anticipation.

As Ben opened his mouth again, craving for water, she got up and put fresh water into the tiny glass to give him more drops with the swab. When she returned, she found Marsha sitting at Ben's bedside, holding his hand.

Suzan put the glass on the sideboard, told Marsha to give him some water and left.

37

When Suzan returned to the studio in the late afternoon, she found Linda sitting on the green armchair, reading a book. Linda behaved like a hostess and asked her if she would fancy a relaxing tea. She had brought some with her.

"Yes, I'd love a relaxing tea," Suzan replied with disguised irony. As they had their tea sitting opposite each other, Suzan kept glancing at Ben, now naked under a white bed sheet.

Linda showed Suzan the book she was reading: *Welcoming Death*.

"I am going to read it after my supper," she said, a smile lighting her small, insecure face. She implied she was well prepared.

A note was left by the nurse. It said that Ben was now under sedation and his body was closing down, withdrawing. At this stage he wouldn't need any water and they shouldn't give him any.

Suzan had given him plenty of water that morning with the swabs, and the note was obviously targeted at her. But Suzan was glad that she had given him water and offered him a last drop of pleasure.

Linda complained about Betty,

"Oh, she is so nervous and forgetful. Last Tuesday she made me wait here till eight o'clock, although I told her that I had a job interview next morning and had to leave at six. I was very annoyed with her."

"Do you know that Betty wants to send another picture to Gisela and Reinhard?" Suzan said.

"Yes, I know about it. I think Ben was very fond of them."

"He was not!" Suzan protested, "In fact he dreaded their company! He hated their lifestyle. And they took advantage of his illness!"

"But I think we must all be kind to each other now," Linda offered with a soft authority. "Ben wanted us to get on well with each other and we must behave the way he wished."

"No!" Suzan said, "I will not behave in the way he wished. I'll remain truthful to myself."

Linda's smile froze and there was uneasiness, even fear, in her small eyes. She turned her face towards the kitchen and said playfully.

"Can you smell my food in the oven?"

Suzan was speechless.

"I think my food is ready now," Linda said in a distant tone of voice. "I brought beef stew from home. I'm going to have it now." She obviously expected Suzan to respect her wish to be left alone.

Suzan, worn out and somehow disoriented, was suddenly intimidated by Linda's quiet power. Unable to judge yet the implications of Linda's wish to be left alone in the studio, she even showed a gesture of hospitality and said, "You can later come and sleep at my house."

"Oh, thank you," Linda grinned, "but I think I prefer to stay here. I brought my laptop with me; I might as well do some work. But I may come and sleep in your house tomorrow."

"As you wish. But I'll give you my spare key, just in case." Suzan left the key on the table, rose to her feet and went to Ben's bed. "How he suffered last night and this morning," she sighed. "Although he was unconscious, he talked to me."

"I'm glad," Linda said in a false enthusiasm.

Suzan left. Only walking down the High Street did she realise that Linda had tactfully expelled her and invaded her place, just as Marsha had done this morning. What a cruel competition was going on. What was it they still wanted? To be the one who would hold Ben's hand at his last breath?

38

Suzan woke up to the sound of a downpour, the water streaming down the street. It felt as if all the pressure, all the anger contained in the sky was now unleashed. The danger of flooding, which had been feared because of high tides and the eclipse of the sun, had now passed; the high pressure had continued during the high tide, and the wind remained light and steady. Had the flood occurred, it could have been the most damaging flood in forty years, everybody being swept away.

At four-thirty the telephone rang. Suzan knew why.

"I'm a Macmillan nurse. I'm sorry, your husband died half an hour ago."

The woman's voice was so motherly that it made Suzan feel like an abandoned child.

"He is very peaceful now," the nurse went on. "Linda is coming to collect you."

"I... think..." Suzan broke off, "I think I'd rather be left alone for a while."

"I am afraid Linda is already on her way to your house," the nurse said. "I am so sorry. He is at peace now."

"Thank you," Suzan said in a trembling whisper. "Thank you very much."

She went downstairs, sat in the dark parlour and listened to the sound of the water streaming down the street. She began to cry.

Then she heard the click of the lock. Linda had the key, Suzan had given it to her. Linda came in and knelt before her:

"Don't be sad."

Suzan looked at Linda, through the veil of tears and it struck her that there was exhilaration rather than sadness in Linda's expression.

"When did he die?" Suzan asked, wiping her tears with the back of her hand.

"At four," Linda answered in a whisper.

"I wish I had been there," said Suzan, trying not to be reproachful, for it was not the time for reproach, nor envy, nor jealousy. Her sadness was so pervasive and possessive that it did not let any other feeling creep in.

"He died happily," Linda offered, as if expecting Suzan to be thankful that she had given Ben comfort in his last moments.

"Let's go there," Suzan said.

The only sound in the deserted street was the roaring of the rubbish lorry parked on the edge of the road, its yellow lights blinking. The rain had stopped. The sky had cleared and the moon was no longer full.

"I told him about you," Linda spoke sweetly.

Suzan did not ask Linda what she had told Ben about her. What could she tell him about her?

Linda sounded so contented that Suzan felt herself silly walking beside her, with tearful eyes, sniffling.

Mozart's 'Requiem' reached them as they crossed the yard. The powerful music vibrated in the dark. Suzan stopped to listen. For a moment she felt thankful to Linda for being with her at this saddest moment of her life.

The nurse, a plump woman with short grey hair, was standing bent over the table, busy with some paperwork.

"Hello," she said softly to Suzan. The tenderness of her voice intensified Suzan's grief and she sobbed uncontrollably.

A candle was lit at his bedside. A pink towel was rolled and put underneath his chin, encircling half of his face.

Suzan sat on the chair next to him and put her hand on his forehead, cool, but not yet cold. It was the most dignified face she had ever seen in her life, Suzan felt, the calmest.

"You are so beautiful," she whispered, unable to take her eyes off him.

The nurse came and bent over to her, "I know it is no consolation for you, but it was the most peaceful death I have ever seen. Try not to be sad."

Suzan nodded and thanked the nurse.

The nurse left. Suzan heard Linda chuckle as she was seeing the nurse off. Then Linda came in and sat on the other side of the bed. The music stopped.

"I put Mozart's Requiem on soon after he died. I knew he liked this music," Linda explained.

"I am glad you were here," Suzan said. "Maybe you were the best company for him right then. I'd have disturbed him with my crying."

"He held my hand tightly," Linda said, a gleam of vanity in her eyes. Was she feeling glad that she had become the last woman to hold his hand and hear his last breath? She had that privilege now and no one could take it away from her. She had to come down just on the right day, his last in this world. Did she know it was his last night? The nurse, who had called in the afternoon, must have told her. But Linda had kept it secret from Suzan. Was this because she wanted to be alone with him? To capture him at a moment when it was impossible for him to sneer at her, to reject her? She had hoped to impress him, to be with him for many years. Now the union had taken place irrevocably. She had taken possession of him.

"I dozed off a few times, while reading my book and instructed the nurse to wake me up when the time came," Linda told Suzan in a wistful tone. "I had prepared everything beforehand: the poem I would read aloud to him, 'While the angel of death came to collect his soul', Mozart's Requiem he loved, and the candle. The nurse woke me up in time and I sat in the chair beside him, read the poem, stroked his forehead and with my other hand I grasped his hand. His hand closed in mine."

"Perhaps he thought it was me," Suzan said tentatively.

"The nurse said 'talk to him, he will hear you.' So I talked to him for ten minutes. Yes, I am sure he was thinking of you. You are the one he loved best."

"We loved each other," Suzan said.

"When he stopped breathing I said to him, 'Dear Ben, you will be at peace now, all the anger has gone out of you.' It was never easy to communicate with him, you know. But in the end I think we communicated very well." Linda smiled broadly at these last words.

Suzan wished to be left alone with him now. But Linda was in a talkative mood.

"The nurse was fascinated when she came in. She said it was the most amazing place she had ever been in. She liked your portraits very much."

Suzan thought no one would ever paint another portrait of her and she felt a pang of regret, thinking she had not thanked him for doing her portraits.

Leaving Linda in the studio, she returned home.

She sat by the window with a cup of tea in her hand. She thought that when one witnesses death, one understands how good it is to have a cup of tea, how beautiful the view outside is, even if it is only a wall, a tree, an angle of the sky. When one witnesses death, one understands how precious every movement, every sensation is. When one witnesses death, all the hatred inside one subsides. If everybody would caress the cool forehead of a dead person, all weapons would be laid down and all wars would cease.

A motorbike came to a halt in the street and interrupted her thoughts, its roar slowly fading… The memory of those Friday mornings hit Suzan. She used to listen alertly to his shabby motorbike stopping outside around ten. She could recognize the sound, an almost methodical sound, unique and peculiar to him. His arrival would be the climax of her week. The coffee cups would be ready in the kitchen, the espresso machine turned on, the fire lit, flowers put on the dining table. And she would be wearing her best clothes, her hair carefully styled. She would rush to the door praying he would be in a good mood, knowing his mood would determine whether they would be the happiest or the most miserable couple in the world. But there was no way to predict his mood. It had no apparent causality and its mystery was impenetrable. Yes, every Friday morning at around ten, the sound of Ben's motor bike coming to a halt outside the house would fill her both with fear and exhilaration. But that motorbike would never stop outside the house again, and she would never again hear the fading roar of that shabby Honda below her window. Her torturer had gone out of her life; the shouts, the sleepless nights, the pervasive smell of alcohol, the shocks, the chain of betrayals, all gone… Wiped out. Her torturer had gone, the man who had made her pay dearly for love. Her torturer had gone and so had her great happiness of being with him.

She phoned Anthony to give him the news. Anthony said he would be in the studio shortly. When Suzan went to the studio, Linda opened the door to her. A black ribbon was tied on the door handle. The undertaker, a tall man dressed in black, was sitting at the table, scribbling in a notebook. Anthony came from the dim recess of the studio and took Suzan into his arms. He drew her to his large, bony chest. Suzan, leaning her face on his chest, burst into tears again. Then she released herself from his strong arms and gazed towards the bed where the dead body lay, feeling somehow guilty of indulging herself in Anthony's comforting embrace. She walked to the bed and felt as if she herself had suffered the unbearable pain in that bed, and that pain had now gone.

His eyes were slightly open now and looked sore, as if frozen tears had accumulated in them. His powerful intense eyes were now deserted by life.

The undertaker finished with the formalities and as he shook hands with Suzan, he said: "And you are?"

"Suzan Somariba, his ex-wife," Linda chimed in eagerly.

After the man left, Suzan asked Anthony and Linda if they would like coffee.

"Yes, that'd be nice," they said simultaneously.

"Oh, we both have brown jackets!" Linda pointed gleefully to Suzan's jacket, and then to hers, hanging on the back of a chair.

Suzan remained aloof.

As they were having coffee sitting at the table, Anthony lapsed into an entertaining mood and said that the other day Polly, his neighbour, had brought him an apple crumble.

"And when June, my wife, came to see me the next day, I offered her some. She asked who made it. I said I did, but she didn't believe me, so then I told her that Polly had made it."

Anthony chuckled and Linda joined him. Suzan looked at Anthony, incredulous of his naïveté. It seemed to her that despite his shining vitality and perfect shape, Anthony was inferior to the dead man who lay there. It occurred to her that she might suffer more from Anthony's cunning mediocrity than she had from Ben's destructive greatness.

Linda explained that Betty had to go to the hospital because of her backache, "When Betty comes back from the hospital, we must go and buy some new clothes for Ben," Linda offered with a clever tone.

Suzan objected to this, saying that Ben would not have liked new clothes. Anthony backed her.

"Okay," Linda gave in. "Then we must choose some clothes for him from downstairs. What do you think he would have liked to wear?"

"A dark blue suit and a white collarless shirt," Suzan replied without hesitation.

"But he can't have a cravat if he has a collarless shirt." It was from Anthony.

"He never wore cravats," Suzan frowned slightly. "He only wore bow ties or a scarf."

Linda went over to Ben's bedside and fumbled zealously with folded cotton handkerchiefs piled on the shelf. Then she lifted out a red handkerchief with red spots. "This?" she smirked.

"No!" Suzan protested. "He would only wear a silk scarf."

"I remember," Linda said, leaving Ben's bedside and addressing Anthony, "when we went together to Truro, Ben ordered a tweed suit at a local tailor. I think he would have liked to wear that suit for his funeral."

Suzan sighed, looking away, and a great weariness pressed upon her. Linda, on the other hand, seemed very animated, eager to make decisions concerning Ben. Now he was in her hands. His dead body, his possessions, his art.

"He always loved fine clothes," Linda expounded.

"But last winter I saw him in a Mackintosh he bought in a second-hand shop," Anthony argued playfully. "He advised me to go to the same shop and buy a similar coat for myself. I went there, but none was big enough for me, so I didn't buy one." Grinning, he glanced at Suzan, as if puzzled by her gravity.

"Let's go downstairs and choose the clothes together, shall we?" Linda offered, coming closer to Suzan, wanting to motivate her.

"Yes, go downstairs and choose his clothes together," Anthony spoke in avuncular intermediary tone of voice.

"All right," Suzan mumbled.

But before going downstairs, she went to Ben's bed again. She looked closely at his half-opened eyes, as if still seeking an eye contact with him. But the most beautiful eyes she had ever seen, the eyes of a ruthless charmer and relentless artist, were now extinguished forever.

She wiped a tear, as she murmured, "His eyes should be closed."

"Usually they use wet cotton to clean the eyes and keep them closed." Linda spoke in an expert tone.

"You must do it so then," Suzan said.

"Anthony, could you clean his eyes with some wet cotton, please?" Linda said to Anthony with gentle authority.

"Yes. Of course." Anthony prepared to perform the ritual.

Suzan felt thankful and yet hurt by Anthony's detached pragmatism.

When Linda unlocked the downstairs studio, a familiar fragrance struck Suzan. This fragrance always pervaded wherever he settled down. A sensuous and reassuring smell, the smell of wood, of turpentine, of earth, the smell of his excitement, his enthusiasm. She would miss that smell.

Everything in the wardrobe and the chest of drawers was clean and tidy.

As Suzan searched through his suits, she came upon an orange silk blouse with black spots on it. It was a woman's blouse, unworn and placed carefully among his elegant suits.

"He probably bought it for me," she murmured, tears welling up.

Linda glanced at the blouse and said, "I think it's too small for you." She probably wanted to keep the blouse for herself. She did not know that all Suzan wanted at this moment was to believe that it was of her that Ben had thought when he had bought this blouse, and had forgotten to give it to her.

Linda diverted Suzan's attention, showing her a pair of yellow socks, "Look, I think he should wear these! I know he liked these socks very much."

Suzan glanced up at Linda in disbelief. What a diabolic soul was hidden behind this angelic and kind facade.

Finally Linda decided Ben should wear his brownish tweed and asked Suzan to choose underpants for him, as though trying to establish some equality between them.

39

The weather was pleasantly warm for mid-September and they were sitting in an open air café by Portlando harbour. A small village overwhelmed by the ocean, by the massive green land. The grey granite tower clock at the end, the green hillside with a few granite cottages, the darkened walls of the quay, the skyline clear, a rowing boat, seagulls perched on the top of the walls, all Suzan saw was now impregnated by him, his painter's sensitivity.

"I was brought up very religiously." Linda interrupted Suzan's contemplation. "But I've taken an interest in other forms of spirituality in recent years, although I still believe in the significance of Jesus," Linda went on, turning her beaming face toward the sea, her delicate hands holding the porcelain cup tightly, "I think Ben too was a spiritual man, although he was annoyed whenever I talked about spirituality. But I think his paintings are spiritual. What do you think? I think his paintings are beyond the material world."

Suzan nodded abstractedly and said: "He was certainly psychic. He could predict what was going to happen. Also his eyes had psychic power, he could influence and direct you with his very look."

"Oh yes! I know that!" Linda gave a gentle laugh. "You know, I was sometimes frightened of his look. And to be honest, he often intimidated me. Made me feel inferior."

Suzan turned her gaze toward the sea, waves crashing against the high dark walls. They both stared into the distance, thinking of Ben whose body now lay in a chapel.

Linda was anxious to talk about the funeral. She asked Suzan with whom she would like to sit during the service.

"I don't know…" Suzan mumbled, still staring at the sea, pondering. Then she turned her face swiftly to Linda and said: "Not with Marsha in any case."

"Why not?" Linda gave an amused smile.

Suzan described the scene with Marsha competing with her to sit on Ben's bed the day before Ben's death. "She was quite bossy and behaved in a ridiculous manner."

"Maybe she meant well," Linda offered in a discretely imposing tone, "But anyway Ben wished that we would all be nice to each other and I believe we should be nice to one another."

"But I don't want to be nice," Suzan snapped, slightly bending over, trying to shake off Linda's ungrounded superior air.

Linda was taken aback and her grin froze for a moment, then, shifting the ground, she gave in: "Okay we will see that Marsha sits in another row." She scrutinised Suzan, expecting appreciation. "By the way," she resumed, "we are distributing Ben's personal belongings. We thought you would like to have his pink Georgian mug. You always had your tea in that, I noticed." She grinned anxiously, "But I will take the green mug, Ben's favourite. Is that okay?"

Suzan, somehow bewildered by this negotiation, nodded abstractedly and said as if talking to herself, "I gave him tea in that cup every afternoon over the last two months."

Linda stared at her, her kind expression fading. Then, eyes cast down, she fumbled with her teaspoon. Then she lifted her face in an attempt at being in command, "Is there anything else you'd like to have?"

Suzan was silent for a while, then staring into the distance, she said, "When we divorced, he took everything he wanted from our mutual home. And we never argued about such things. Now I don't want to take anything from his studio."

"Okay." Linda looked down to disguise her amazement and her sense of relief. "I understand."

"But I would like to know what would happen to Tamarisk?"

"Oh, Tamarisk!" Linda's face lit up with a wistful smile, "I love Tamarisk. I think everybody loves Tamarisk. I shall come and stay myself there for a while, maybe with my partner. But then Ben's friends will be welcome to come and stay sometimes, to remember him, to keep his memory alive."

Suzan fixed a cold glance at Linda, determine not to share her sentimentality. Silent moments passed. Then she said: "But who has inherited Tamarisk? That's legally. I would like to know."

"Nobody," Linda replied assertively then she called for the waitress to pay for their coffee and her chocolate cake.

"Thank you," Suzan mumbled.

"My pleasure," Linda smiled eagerly.

As they walked side by side to her car, parked opposite the café, she asked somehow cautiously, "Would you mind if Betty and I sit with you at the funeral?"

"No," said Suzan. "Oh, by the way," she added, "there are three books in the studio which belong to the public library. I forgot to take them back. Could you drop them at the library?"

"I'm very busy at the moment," Linda replied in a distant tone. "I don't think I'll have time to do that."

"Okay. I'll come and collect them," Suzan paused, "But I can't enter the studio these days. It's very difficult for me to go there and not to see Ben." She fought back tears, then spoke in a low voice, "I became addicted to our sad meetings during these last months."

"I understand," Linda said kindly.

There was silence.

"By the way, what are you going to do with the place?" Suzan asked.

"It's so beautifully arranged," said Linda, "So I think I might use the studio for a while myself. The rent is quite cheap."

Suzan did not know what to say, how to react to Linda's arbitrary decision. Linda seemed quite conscientious over the power she had suddenly gained.

"Is your boyfriend coming for the funeral?" Suzan asked, to change the subject.

"No!" Linda moaned. "He can't. It's a long journey and he is working. But we speak on the phone every day. I am glad I have someone I can give my love and affection to now."

Suzan said nothing but wondered if Linda had really loved Ben, or was that a mere excitement, elevation she felt at knowing such an extraordinary man. Did any of those women fascinated by him love him in the way she had? Certainly none of them came close to his wild, fiery, destructive and yet generous soul as much as she did.

As they drove to town, "Can I come and stay in your place tomorrow?" Linda asked ingratiatingly, "So we can go to the funeral together?"

"Of course. You are welcome," Suzan replied flatly.

"Oh, thank you!" Linda's voice tinkled.

She dropped Suzan at the side of the busy road opposite the studio. She was in a hurry, she explained. She had to meet Betty at the studio. Then together they would go to the chapel where Ben's body lay and to the cemetery to see whether everything was properly arranged.

40

That afternoon Sam, Ben's friend for many years, phoned Suzan from Holland. Suzan had previously spoken a few times with Sam over the phone.

"I was wrecked yesterday, when I heard the news," Sam said, "Such a loss. It must be very hard for you. You know… I wanted to come and spend some time with him, but he rejected me. We have known each other for forty years."

"He was afraid of emotions," said Suzan and said no more.

"I heard you were reconciled and together," Sam's voice tinkled.

"Yes. We were… I think we became closer than ever before."

There was a moment of silence on the line. Then Sam said, "Thank you for being with him. By the way, could you do something for me?"

"What is it?"

"Could you order a bouquet of white carnations for the funeral. I will send you a cheque."

"Of course, I'll do that. But don't send me a cheque."

"Thank you. Take care."

After the call, Suzan went straight to the flower shop to order two bouquets – one for Sam, one for herself. She wanted her bouquet to be of a dozen red roses, the symbol of Ben's English taste.

The florist, a plump, efficient young woman, asked her to choose a card, "Was he your friend?"

"He was my husband," Suzan replied quietly.

"Oh, I am sorry!" the woman gasped. And she asked her what her late husband was called.

"Ben," Suzan said.

After fumbling with cards, the woman chose the one with the words, 'To my dearest husband,' on it.

"No, not this one," Suzan said gently. "I want that one." She pointed to the card with the words: 'To a very special person'.

As Suzan was leaving, the woman said emphatically, "I am really sorry. He was a lovely man. I remember seeing you two together. I always thought what a happy couple."

"Yes," Suzan nodded. "Thank you."

41

Linda came carrying a glossy carrier bag.

"You are an hour late," Suzan reproached gently, as she opened the door.

"Why?" Linda was defensive.

"You said seven."

"No, I said between seven and eight!" Linda insisted, which was not true.

"Anyway, come into the kitchen. I have cooked a stew and the table is set."

As soon as she entered the kitchen, Linda thrust her hand into the bag, while giving Suzan a look of intrigue. Then she took out a tiny box of strawberries,

"Here are some strawberries for you! Organic!" she announced gleefully.

Her gesture irritated Suzan and she noticed that the strawberries were not fresh, but overripe and flabby. That meant they were not bought for her; probably Linda had bought them for herself and forgotten to eat them. But Suzan had no choice but to accept the offer.

"Thank you."

"Oh, I am starving!" Linda exclaimed, "It smells so good!"

"I was intending to set the table in the lounge, but because you were late, I decided we would eat in the kitchen," Suzan said.

"Oh I like eating in the kitchen, it's cosier," Linda said with a contrived grin.

Suzan served the meal and they started eating,

"It's delicious!" Linda enthused. "What kind of spice did you put in it?"

Suzan had no wish to talk about food. She wanted to ask Linda about the money she was supposed to receive.

"I have been to my solicitor today," she said coolly.

"Good. And? Are you… satisfied?" Linda tilted her head.

"No, I'm not."

"Oh. I am sorry," Linda feigned a kind of compassion, "Can you tell me why are you not satisfied?"

"Well, you must know why?" Suzan was abrupt, and after a pause she resumed, "Ben told me that I am to receive £10,000 immediately. And this money is not there."

"There is no such money." Linda looked away.

"But why then did Ben tell me that I am to receive that money immediately? And I know him very well. He wouldn't lie to me, not on such matters anyway."

Linda lowered her eyes and her small mouth tightened. After a moment of silence, regaining her self-control, she spoke in a business-like manner: "I wish the money were available. And I wish I could help you out. But I don't have enough money myself."

"I don't want any money from you," Suzan mumbled. "You might not know but I have never discussed with him about his inheritance until he mentioned it to me. But now, I believe I deserve his inheritance more than anyone else. And… by the way, I did not have an easy life with him."

"Yes, but you must try to think positively now," Linda interrupted in a gentle, yet patronising tone. "He loved you. He loved you more than he did anybody else, and you must admit you have also been happy together. I personally always try to be constructive in relationships with people rather than destructive. And I would like all of us to get on well now. I have a great responsibility. And I will see that you are well provided for. And Ben told me so."

Suzan seized the opportunity to challenge Linda directly.

"I guess Ben told you to give me £10,000 in cash. But you may have decided to keep the money for expenses. Is that so?"

"No. Ben told me nothing about £10,000 cash," Linda's voice was bitter now. "And I wouldn't lie to you."

"But when we were talking in the garden, remember? When you came down to Cornwall two weeks ago, that Ben wanted to leave me £10,000 cash? But you said, 'More than that.'"

"I didn't say that," Linda denied, "I don't recall that we talked about money at all."

"But I recall it very clearly."

"Anyway, his money in the bank is frozen by law, we can't touch it."

"But Ben must have known about the law," Suzan persevered, "He must have known that the money in the bank would be frozen after his death. He was a methodical man and organized everything beforehand."

"I know," Linda smiled wistfully. "And believe me, I will do all I can to help you." She patted Suzan's hand.

Suzan's doubts did not subside.

After a moment's silence, she said, "And I find it strange that Marsha's sons, Andy and Ben have the same share as me from the estate. These two boring young men. For some reason Ben always rewarded people who bored him. It was his masochism, I suppose."

Linda smiled sadly.

"I think I bored him too. Whenever I talked to him, he always glared at me."

"But he liked you," Suzan lied, not wanting to hurt her.

"Oh, thank you!" Linda exclaimed, "I am glad to hear that. And I am going to do my best to make him famous."

She leaned back and started nibbling at the strawberries which Suzan had served in a porcelain bowl. Suzan had no appetite for them perhaps because she saw them as the symbol of Linda's deceitfulness.

"Oh, I am looking forward to the funeral," Linda offered with an expression of exhilaration. Then, glancing up at Suzan, she added, "Does that sound strange?"

Suzan shook her head but said nothing.

"I am going to wear my black flannel trousers," Linda resumed, "What do you think? Is it inappropriate to wear trousers to a funeral?" Leaning her elbows on the table, she tilted her head toward Suzan in feminine intimacy.

"Wear what you want." Suzan looked down.

"I am going to buy a hat tomorrow morning," Linda went on cheerfully, ignoring Suzan's remoteness, "Would you like to come with me, so you can help me with the choice?"

"I can't. I must prepare myself for the funeral. Emotionally…"

"I understand," Linda nodded solemnly.

She helped Suzan to clear the table and insisted on washing up.

"You know, Andy and Ben were so relaxed and funny in the studio today," she expounded as she fumbled with a dirty plate in the soapy water. "I never saw them so relaxed before. I think they were intimidated by Ben when he was alive. Perhaps we were all a bit intimidated by him."

Suzan sat back on her chair and looking out of the window, her tired eyes resting on the silhouette of the garden wall overhung with trellis. 'Yes, she thought resentfully, They were all intimidated by him. And they could not get close to him.

42

Suzan found Linda sitting in the lounge early the next morning. She looked vulnerable and delicate in her white fibre underwear – half sleeved T-shirt and shorts. She was busy sewing the torn shoulder of the black velvet jacket Suzan would wear to the funeral. And this unsolicited generosity made Suzan feel indebted to her. She prepared a special breakfast for her with cereals, mushrooms, eggs and tomatoes.

Linda was delighted. As she ate her cereals, she elapsed into a chit-chat mood again.

"I was so busy over the few days, I forgot to cut my fingernails, and I didn't bring my nail clippers with me. Look how horrible they are." She stretched out her elegant, white hands.

Suzan gave her a reproachful look, but Linda persevered, "They break easily. Probably I need to eat more dairy products. But I don't drink milk any more. Maybe I should."

In suppressed exasperation, Suzan looked away, longing for silence, but Linda went on talking: "Oh, these cereals are really good, very generous with nuts and raisins."

"Would you like to come with me to Portlando to the hat shop?" Linda finally said, like an adult offering a diversion to a grumpy child.

"No, thanks."

"Are you okay?" Linda brought her face close to Suzan's.

"Yes. Yes, I'm okay, a bit disorientated." Suzan sighed.

"Do you want to try my foot oil? I bought it from the health food shop. It makes you feel grounded."

"No, thank you. I don't want to try anything new now. I just want to be quiet."

"Oh! It was a delicious breakfast," Linda enthused, "Thank you. What do you think of my blouse? It's brown, not black. I hope it looks all right? The reason I didn't buy the hat yesterday was because I wanted to match it with my blouse and flannel trousers." She got up and adopted an efficient air: "Right, I shall be off now. I'll be back at half past twelve and at half past one I can drive you to the cemetery."

After Linda had gone, Suzan realised more than ever before how tiring it was to be with Linda, to listen to her. What a tedium it must have been to spend time with that woman.

Linda returned with her new hat on, beaming, eager to hear Suzan's opinion.

"What do you think?"

"It's nice," Suzan forced a smile.

"Guess who I met in Portlando?" Linda tilted her head, grinning. Getting no response from Suzan, she added, "Anthony…" She paused, observing Suzan.

"Good," Suzan was not interested.

"We had coffee together in the café where you and I sat the other day," Linda went on, "And we made some plans."

"What plans?" Suzan finally showed some curiosity.

"Plans about Tamarisk."

Hearing that, Suzan stiffened and said, "Tell me."

"Well… I thought after the funeral…"

"Since you have already mentioned, I would like to know now," Suzan spoke firmly.

After a moment of silence Linda said in a rather defiant tone: "Anthony is going to use Ben's studio at Tamarisk. They were good friends, you know."

"Were they?" Suzan said in a whispering tone and looked away.

"Yes. They were!" Linda offered, "And I think Anthony is a… He is a fine man."

"Do you fancy him?" Suzan turned her face to Linda, scrutinizing her fiercely.

"Yeah... I do." Linda replied languidly, "We get on well, I think. We have things in common."

"You mean you both love Tamarisk?" Suzan cut in.

"Oh, we all... everybody loves Tamarisk. I think I'll spend a lot of time there in the future."

"Good," Suzan muttered, seized by anger, but feeling also powerless towards Linda's discretely growing power she added, "Mind you, I want to be completely quiet until the funeral."

"Yes. Of course. I understand," Linda said in a whispering tone. "We have to be at the chapel ten minutes before the ceremony."

Suzan went upstairs to dress. When she looked in the mirror Suzan found herself regretting that she hadn't worn this outfit – a black velvet skirt suit with this hat while Ben was still alive. He would certainly have flattered her. She had to learn to live on without his flatteries now, without the rewarding look of his intense eyes.

When she came down, Linda cheered, "Oh, you look so pretty! I like your curls." She pointed to the curls under Suzan's small black velvet hat.

"Thanks," Suzan mumbled looking down.

43

A small group of young men were gathered outside the cemetery gate. Marsha's two sons Andy and Ben, dressed in black, were among them. They were all chatting animatedly and looked like men waiting for a football match or a rock concert.

Suzan stayed on the other side of the gate waiting for the coffin to arrive while Linda joined the group. She found herself defending her privacy more than ever before. What she now felt was not to be shared with anybody around her, not to be conveyed in words.

The black funeral car arrived. When Suzan's eyes caught sight of the pale wooden coffin with its gilded ornaments and white and red flowers on the lid, she felt what she saw could not be true. And as she saw the men carrying out the coffin from the hearse, a sense of revolt stirred inside her. How could he yield to be put into such a strange box, how could he be so hidden? Where was he? Where was his face, his look? She turned her face to the wall of the cemetery and wept and sobbed. A gentle hand touched her shoulder, "Leave me alone!" she shouted, thinking it was Linda. Turning, she saw a woman dressed in a nun's habit.

"I'm sorry," she mumbled.

"That's okay," the woman whispered, "Cry as much as you want."

She stopped crying. Then Linda came up and led her after the coffin.

As she walked behind it, her eyes rested on the bouquet of red roses on the foot of the coffin. Her roses. Her name was written on it. Suddenly she felt he was taking their love with him.

She entered the chapel, a grey stone building lit with a bluish light.

She was led to her seat in the first row, Linda on her left side and the vicar on her right. Looking at the coffin a revelation came to her that Ben was not in the coffin, not in the chapel. He was inside her. A part of him was settled inside her, the part she loved, the candid, the artist, the hero...

After the hymn and the speech, Suzan was invited to speak. It had been Betty's suggestion. But Suzan could not speak. Her eyes fixed on the coffin, she began to read a poem she wrote for him.

"This world had never been good enough for you,
Never beautiful enough.
So you changed the angles and shifted the symmetry.
You broke, you composed, you magnified.
You competed with trees,
You competed with the colour of the sea
You mixed as you pleased
the shadow and the light.
Like a conqueror you narrowed your eyes,
to see the continent of your dreams.
You were a Romeo and met Juliet in your canvas,
caressed her with your brush.
How many nights in silence,
you climbed up the ladder in the moonlight.
This world had never been good enough for you.
Never beautiful enough.
So you created as many worlds as you wanted.
And after you
we will see in them
what you wanted to see."

A deep silence fell upon the chapel after the rendition, a silence of surprise, of recognition. Now she had come out of the shadow. She thanked the audience briefly in a whispering tone and returned to her seat.

Then Linda rose with a broad smile to read a poem and said in a tone of entertainment that she had read this poem to Ben before he died. She was like those onlookers around a television crew in a public place, eager to show their face to the camera, to stand out from the crowd, hoping to be miraculously discovered.

There was a light breeze but the sun shone brightly as they walked to the grave between rows of old tombstones with faded engravings on them. His grave was at the end of the cemetery. A spot away from the world, calm, modest and yet glamorous in its location. Green hills and a dense wood in the distance, fields of various shades of green. 'He must have liked the view,' Suzan thought to herself.

Waiting at the grave, she was carried away. At that moment, the crowd did not exist for her, no one existed. Even she herself did not exist. The real world did not exist. And the coffin and the grave lost their physical meaning. Then she heard words inside her, words saying: 'The universe is full of death; dead trees, dead butterflies, dead cells within each of us.'

With this thought she was brought back to reality. She fixed her eyes on the coffin as it was lowered into the grave. Her focus was clear now. That was the last sight of him. The last moment of their togetherness.

At a signal from the vicar, she picked up some earth from the tiny box on the edge of the grave. She bent over it, grasped the cool, dry earth, and spilled it over the coffin. She slowly retired, making way for the second mourner, Linda. She turned her eyes away and thought: 'He must have imagined himself in the coffin, surrounded by the flowers, trees, hills, fields with hedges.'

As they walked along the path to the exit, people began coming up to hug Suzan. The postman, the lighthouse keeper, the fisherman, the shopkeepers, the housewives, all giving her hearty, clumsy hugs, somehow apologetic for their judgements of her and saying,

"I am sorry."

"Oh, it must be very hard for you."

"We all loved him."

Some women leaned on Suzan's shoulders and cried, expecting her to cry with them.

But Suzan was now calm.

Alicia who worked part-time in the pub, and had had an affair with Ben, cried, too, "I went to the chapel yesterday," she said, "I visited him. He didn't look like himself at all. I searched for his hand and had difficulty finding it. I touched him and talked to him. I loved him though I knew he was a selfish bastard." Alicia squeezed Suzan's hand and with tears running down her cheeks, she smiled warmly. Suzan tried to smile back.

Linda drove Suzan to the studio for the wake. Suzan was unable to behave like a hostess, because she was no longer. Linda and Betty were. She was a guest. She had always been a guest. Perhaps Ben had made him feel so. And all the friendly local people around her too. But they were all kind to her now. Death wiped out all judgements even if temporarily.

Lisa wearing a large, velvet hat, her eyelids and cheeks swollen by a regular intake of Barley Wine came and sat on the green armchair.

"You handled it graciously," she said, "I am proud of you. How are you feeling?"

"I am feeling well," Suzan said.

"Maybe too well," Lisa said, looking at her with a doubt in her sly eyes, "You look very tired, my dear, you look drained. I never saw you so sad. You look terrible. Shall I come and stay with you tonight? Or do you want to come and stay with us? Anyway you know where I am."

"I am all right, Lisa, really. I don't mind being alone."

Lisa's dubious stare lingered on Suzan's face for a long moment.

The ham and cheese sandwiches were consumed in no time and the whisky and sherry bottles quickly emptied. The hand-made wooden bed, with no one in, was overlooked. Only Suzan could see him still lying there. She recalled how she lifted him, how she helped him cross the room, backing him up from behind. She remembered how close they had become in those quiet, deserted nights.

The next day she was hit by grief. She had no wish to get up, to eat, to go out, all her energy drained. She felt as if she would no longer know what to do, where to go, how to live, how to work, how to meet people and how to love. She found herself envying him in his grave, in an immaculate tranquillity in the middle of green fields.

44

The sky was grey and overcast the next day. But Suzan was determined to walk to Tamarisk rather then wait for a bus or take a taxi. It would take her four hours to get there and she didn't mind. She needed a long walk. She needed to go to Tamarisk.

She was wearing her hooded green anorak, and walking boots. She walked on the high street like a sleep walker, hardly discerning people and descended the stone steps behind the monument to get quickly to Portlando valley. As she crossed the wood, it drizzled and the smell of pine trees mingled with the smell of sea weeds.

After reaching the cliff path, she sped up, anxious to reach her target before an outbreak of rain. 'Is he watching this view too?' she asked herself, 'watching with the eyes of a painter? His eyes will never disappear.' And yes, she felt as though she was watching the view both through her own eyes and his.

As she climbed towards the hill, the wind whipped at her, propelling her forwards. She walked along the narrow footpath, struggling to keep her balance in the increasing wind. She came across the three horses. As she passed close to them, fear rushed through her. The horses might be disturbed by her closeness and attack her. She could lose her balance, already hard to maintain in the gusty wind, and she could fall off the high cliff onto the massive rocks. For a brief moment she found herself wishing it. That would be a glamorous finale, she thought sadly. Such death would suit her better than dying after a long bed-ridden illness. That would be like the finale scene of an opera. She would be washed away by the sea and disappear. Of course he would come to meet her, somewhere during her itinerary. But suddenly her dream came to her mind pumping energy through her.

She passed close to the horses; there was no other way and she could not turn back. Looking straight ahead, she walked on. As she had anticipated, one of the horses grabbed the collar of her jacket from behind. But a sense of extraordinary detachment came over her, and the horse let go of her. She walked on and on. Heather and meadow-sweet decorated the thick fresh grass and seagulls were perched on the dark rocky cliffs. Only when she saw the chimneys of the house did she stop and tears ran down her burning cheeks.

The roof was now repaired, the chimney rebuilt, walls decorated. Maybe he knew she would move there after selling the cottage. Maybe he wanted her to move there. She would be the most suitable inhabitant of Tamarisk after he had gone.

Suzan found the floor wet with rising damp, and mildew on everything.

That night, the wind was roaring across the dark moor, and seagulls were screaming in chorus. On her first night alone, she was overcome by the intense solitude.

She was too frightened to climb up the heavy wooden ladder which lead to the bedroom, and slept instead on the bench in the kitchen. But with the arrival of daylight, a calm settled over her.

The next day was sunny. She went to the spring and filled the two porcelain jugs, carried in wood and coal from the garden. She left the outside doors open to fight the damp and she spread the bed sheets and blankets over the garden wall. Sitting by the window at dusk, and watching the moor slowly sink into the thickening darkness, a voice inside her told her to stay in this house.

The following night was very quiet, no wind, no rain. She could hear the buzzing of a fly, the flutter of a butterfly, the noise of a piece of plaster dropping from the ceiling. She decided to sleep in the double bed up the ladder.

That night he rode on a white horse and crossed the vast moor to come to Tamariskt. And he climbed up the ladder. She took him in his arms and their souls slept in the same body.

*

He was digging the garden energetically. He asked her to pick the weeds. "We'll have a good summer," he said and pointed, "Plenty of lettuces, look here!"

*

They sat in a large hall amidst a silent crowd absorbed in preparations. These were preparations for Ben's death.

Suzan standing behind Ben, combed carefully his hair; thinking he must have his hair done before he is taken to the land of death. And his hair was thick, dark and long, dropping like a solid substance.

*

Then they danced to celebrate his approaching death. They danced with happy slowness, holding each other and smiling, they turned round and round. Other couples danced too, to a silent music, the music of death.

*

An old black Mercedes was sent to take him to the land of death. He sat between two women in the back. Suzan sat in front with the driver. She knew the destination was death. She heard him give instructions to one of those two women, who turned out to be Linda and Betty, about what should be done after his death. Hearing him say 'my death' Suzan buried her face in her hands and began to cry.

*

Her father was standing in front of her and she stretched out her hand to say goodbye but he insisted on kissing her on the cheeks. She was reluctant, because his face was painted grey and was like a cement mask. She was afraid the paint would go off on her face, too, but it didn't. Then her father took off the mask and Suzan saw that it was Ben.

*

Suzan went out into the garden and saw a huge flower with purple and white petals. Then Ben came up and she showed it to him. The flower grew and expanded in their hands and became a painting.

"Shall we hang it on the wall?" asked Suzan.

"If you wish," he said.

They went in and pondered on which wall to hang it.

Suzan showed a broken, ruined wall in the kitchen. They hung the picture on this wall, thus covering the hollowness of the destroyed wall.

*

Ben took her to an unknown town. He was as usual wearing his Irish tweed coat and cloth cap. He was very thin because of his illness, but jolly and in good spirit. Holding hands, they walked along steep, narrow streets bordered by small granite cottages, huddled together. Flowerpots were in their windows, and on their balconies.

They passed through a cobbled alleyway. Entered a huge building. Ben paid for their entry and joked with the girl who sold the tickets:

"I don't mind paying to see my paintings," he said and winked to Suzan, squeezing her hand.

He led her up the winding stairs, then into his new studio which had no walls, no ceiling, no floor. But his paintings hung on the invisible walls.

"Did you paint them after your death?" Suzan asked.

"Yes," he whispered, nodding.

Suzan studied them and was surprised to see that they were painted in an impressionist style and depicted crowded open-air cafes and streets.

"Do you like them?" Ben asked widening his eyes.

"Yes!" Suzan said, *"they are like paintings by Cezanne."*

He nodded coyly and pouted: "Hmm…"

They left the building and, holding hands, walked on. As they crossed a square, "I think you are having a remission," Suzan said.

"I'm feeling much better," he replied.

He stopped and chatted with people waiting at a bus stop. Then they resumed their walk and arrived at wasteland at the edge of town. Opposite, was a mustard coloured cement building, probably an office block.

"Look at that monstrosity," Ben said indignantly.

Suddenly, smoke started billowing from the building. Then flames became visible.

"Fire!" Suzan cried, "You set the building on fire with your eyes!"

Ben shrugged, implying innocence.

The building began to explode and pieces flew all around, injuring people who hung about. But Ben and Suzan walked quietly away, heading towards the town of tiny cottages. Then Suzan snuggled up against him, brushing her face against his warm coat and said, "I love you."

*